ARSENIC & ALIBIS

A CORPSE COLLECTOR SERIES

BOOK ONE

TAMMY TYREE

CHLOE HALE

CAST OF CHARACTERS

SERIES MAIN CAST:

Get access to the character cards and book bonuses in The Vault when you subscribe!

https://tammy-tyree.kit.com/2cc3220f59

"ARSENIC & ALIBIS" SUSPECTS AND VICTIMS:

Lydia Grant: Owner of a local cosmetic shop specializing in a world-renowned botanical and natural product beauty line. Originally from Portland, Lydia and her husband, Robert Grant, moved to Castle Point because they wanted a simpler life. She is in direct competition with Marcia Wells, as Marcia is introducing a botanical, organic line of skincare and cosmetics to her Trend Savvy line.

Marcia Wells: Owner of a world-renowned cosmetic line called "Trend Savvy," Marcia has a more modern and aggressive formula and marketing approach. Her customers request cosmetics made with more natural ingredients, so Lydia Grant has become her direct rival.

Robert Grant: Lydia's husband and somewhat disinterested party in the cosmetic business, focusing more on his real estate ventures; he and Lydia still share their home in Castle Point, but they are estranged.

Julian Ravenscroft: A prominent lawyer in Portland and Castle Point's elite, known for his legal prowess and his role in the town's high society. His relationship with Marcia Wells, a beauty industry magnate, intertwines professional and personal spheres.

Elizabeth Vincent: Better known as Liz, is the epitome of ambition veiled by charm. As Marcia Well's cosmetic chemist in Portland's bustling beauty industry, Liz portrays herself as a dedicated and loyal ally.

Victor Venn: An obsessive, cunning genealogist with secrets deeply rooted in the past. He harbors a grudge with Marcia that has festered over generations.

CHAPTER 1
CORPSE COLLECTING

MY EYES FLEW open as my furry alarm clock, Alfie—my gray-striped tabby cat—sat on my chest, his meows broadcasting his breakfast needs. I swear, he's louder than a megaphone-wielding rooster at dawn. I'd probably complain about his persistence, but seeing as he's the only man in my life, I put up with his 'cattitude.' Following the passing of a well-loved Castle Point resident, I welcomed the furry fellow into my home. He exuded an air of distinction, so Alfie seemed a fitting name.

"Okay, handsome fellow." I stroked his short, soft fur, "get off and let me up." Alfie bolted from the bed and, head and tail held high, marched to the kitchen.

Groaning, I followed, staggered into the kitchen, and dropped a generous scoop of kitty kibble into a dish—enough to appease my feline overlord. Once his incessant meowing ceased, I fired up the coffeemaker. As Alfie filled his gaping maw with kitty chow, I sipped on the first, too-hot gulp of my caffeine fix and scalded my mouth, leaving me in caffeinated pain.

Nursing my scorched palate, I stepped onto the tiny back deck into the crisp morning air. My ivy-covered brick home seemed to shimmer under the pale morning light and cast a small shadow across the large heritage-home-turned-business —The Critt Family Funeral Home and Memorial Gardens. I inherited the business from my father, Caspian Critt, who died fifteen years earlier. Sipping my coffee, I savored the morning's tranquility and the gravestones' silence and stillness beyond the fence.

A deep male voice tinged with a lascivious undertone cut through my reverie.

"Mornin', Miss Critt." I froze as reality hit me like a tidal wave - It wasn't a ghost from the grave. It was the neighbor on the other side of me, Horace—an elderly man with a penchant for inappropriate comments.

And I was standing there in all my nightgown-clad glory, reminiscent of an 80-year-old teacup-collecting shut-in.

My *thin* nightgown.

Fiddlesticks! Why couldn't I have been wearing my flannel PJs?

Because they were too hot, and menopause is a thing.

"Horace! For God's sake, man. Keep your literal nose on your side of the fence!"

"But, the view is best on your side." he winked.

I wrapped my arms around my chest, my coffee cup straining under the pressure of my tightly wrapped fist. "I appreciate the compliment, Horace. Now, shoo!"

With lightning speed, I dashed back inside, not before tripping on the edge of the step and spilling coffee down my front. Screeching and pulling the hot fabric away from my sensitive lady parts, I cursed my clumsiness and the uneven steps!

I should be grateful for Horace's compliment, as I received very few. My generous height and size rarely rendered niceties from the male 'sex.' I blushed, even thinking about the word. Not that I'm a prude, but as I mentioned, men view me more like a mastodon in a historical museum than a voluptuous, tall, graceful woman.

Okay, graceful was a stretch. I snorted at the double meaning, nearly blowing hot coffee out my nose. I was often called 'stretch' in high school because I towered over most of the kids in my class. Grabbing a tissue, I blotted at my nose and then my nightdress. It was time to shower and change.

The fact was, I cared little about my looks or tried, with some effort, to accept myself as I was. I took after my father– God rest him– in more ways than my career. He was also a man of substantial height and a tad frumpy with his penchant for elbow-patched sweaters, wool slacks, and thinning drab hair. In looks, I took after my father.

Much to my mother's dismay.

She considered herself an elitist in our small community. She was petite and always perfectly coiffed. More often than not, my mother commented on my plain looks, black wardrobe, and generous size, and her comments were…a tad unsupportive.

My phone rang, jolting me from my state of mid-dress. I answered, only to be met with a crackly voice on the other end. It was Agnes, a seasoned nurse from the local aged care home. She was a sweetheart, but her hearing wasn't what it used to be.

"Carrigan! Can you hear me, dear?" she shouted.

I held the phone away from my ear. Just because she couldn't hear, she assumed nobody else could, either. "I can, Agnes! How are you?" I shouted into the phone, trying not to startle Alfie.

"Oh, I'm just fine, dear. Listen, I'm afraid we've had a passing at the home. Mr. Thompson. Such a lovely man."

I nod, even though she can't see me. "Yes, I remember him; he was a good friend of my father's. It's such a shame, but I suppose it's a blessing after years of having dementia. He'll be missed."

"Yes, too true. When can you retrieve his body? Not to rush you, dear, but others need the room." Agnes, ever the sweet yet practical nurse, said.

"I'll come pick him up as soon as I can." The nature of my business caused me to be both apathetic and level-headed.

Death was, after all, a part of life.

And death was my business.

"Thank you, dear. You're always so kind. And thank you for taking the time. I know you're busy with your... corpse collecting."

I can't help but chuckle at the nickname certain townsfolk called me. "Corpse Collector." It's not the most flattering moniker, but it's fitting, given my line of work. After all, I owned the only funeral home in town, and body removal—'collecting corpses'—was part and parcel of the business.

After hanging up with Agnes, I quickly showered and dressed, opting for my usual black slacks and baggy sweater. As I pulled on my knee-high stockings, I ripped the first pair. As I carefully pulled the second pair into place, I noticed the hair on my legs had grown past stubble to full-blown, stroke-able locks. I hadn't shaved in ages, and it showed.

"Alfie! Remind me to make a waxing appointment!" I called out, knowing full well that he was a terrible note-taker. Maybe these 'Alexa' loving goons were onto something. With a sigh, I carefully slid the stockings on, ensuring I did not snag my last pair.

I slipped on my favorite black flats and gave myself a once-over in the mirror. My hair was messy and a bit sassy, which I loved, but I knew that once it dried, it would return to its poker-straight, limp-lock style.

As I headed out the door, Alfie peered up at me and swatted at his backpack cat carrier. "Oh, don't give me that look, Mister. I have things to do and bodies to attend to, and you know I can't take you with me. I promise to bring you back a treat from the cafe."

He wouldn't take 'no' for an answer. He gripped the carrier's zipper with a surprisingly strong paw and dragged it open. I studied him, mildly terrified and impressed all at the same time. Then, I gave in. "Fine! Get in, you great baboon."

Cursing the carrier and Alfie's previous owner, who trained him to love it, I opened it the rest of the way. Alfie happily jumped inside. The carrier reminded me of a piece of carry-on luggage but with backpack straps and an astronaut-looking bubble poised front and center. He could see all and be seen by all. Great. Now, I would look like a ghostbuster as I collected poor Mr. Thompson.

The drive to the care home was short, and I used the time to mentally prepare for the day ahead. I've always been a multitasker, but juggling various roles could be exhausting. Still, I wouldn't have it any other way.

When I arrived at the care home, Agnes greeted me warmly. "Carrigan, dear, thank you for coming so quickly. And I see you've brought a friend!"

"Of course, Agnes. It's no trouble at all. And yes, Alfie wanted to come to say 'hi.'" Alfie meowed. I slipped the carrier off my back and unzipped it. Alfie popped out and immediately started rubbing up against Agnes's legs. She bent down to pat him, then led me to Mr. Thompson's room.

I took a deep breath as I entered the room, steeling myself for the task ahead. Agnes gently squeezed my arm before leaving me to do my work. I appreciated her understanding; she knew this process required respect and care.

As I prepared Mr. Thompson for transport, I felt a sudden chill in the room. The hairs on the back of my neck stood on end, and I knew without a doubt that Mr. Thompson's spirit was present. Alfie's howl punctuated this as he looked directly at the wall beside me.

I took a deep breath and focused my energy, opening myself to his presence.

"Mr. Thompson," I whispered, "I'm here to help you on your journey. You don't have to be afraid."

The chill intensified. I looked to my left and saw Mr. Thompson's hazy form develop—exactly where Alfie was looking. Alfie meowed as I offered Mr. Thompson a small smile, which he returned.

Mr. Thompson reached out to pet Alfie, who attempted to push himself into Mr. Thompson's ghostly hand. I smiled. It was cool that I had a paranormal companion in my cat—the ghost whisperer.

Mr. Thompson moved his hand to my shoulder. A chill rushed down my arm into my hand. "I'll be seeing Caspian soon, I expect," he said, referring to my father.

"Yes, you will indeed. Please give him my love?" I asked, a tear tickling my cheek.

"Of course, of course. After all these years of suffering a muddled head, I'm happy to be reunited with my friend."

I nodded. "Dementia is a beast of a thing. I know you suffered from it for so long."

"Yes, I'm so glad to be done with that nonsense. It is so difficult to remember things. Important things…"

"I'm glad you're at peace now, Mr. Thompson. Take all the beautiful memories you have with you." I smiled.

Mr. Thompson returned the smile. He turned away from me, looked out the window, then turned back. "Carrigan, something is…I'm remembering…your father…"

My interest was piqued. "Yes…?" I prodded.

"He…he left something with me…for you…so long ago… I was supposed to give it to you, but I didn't. I'm having difficulty remembering…"

Excitement shuddered through me. "Oh! Mr. Thompson, try to remember. What was it?"

His brow wrinkled. Placing a finger to his lips, he muttered, "It's…no, I can't recall. I'm so sorry."

I sighed.

"It's alright, Mr. Thompson. My father would have given it to me directly if it was important."

He nodded, placing his hand on my shoulder once more. "I suspect you're right. Goodbye, Carrigan."

After a few moments, the chill and Mr. Thompson's ghostly form dissipated, and I knew that his spirit had moved on. I took a deep breath, feeling a sense of peace. Knowing I've helped someone find their path to the beyond was always a bittersweet moment.

With a grateful heart, I stuffed Alfie into his carrier and transferred Mr. Thompson's body from the bed to the gurney —quite an easy task for someone my size and strength—and wheeled him out of the room with a nod to Agnes, who'd been waiting patiently in the hallway. She handed me an envelope with Mr. Thompson's requests and his last remaining personal effects, and I wheeled the gurney out of the building and into the hearse.

After a last check to ensure everything was secure, I climbed into the driver's seat and started the engine. As I drove back to the funeral home, I thought about how much had changed in my life since I turned 40.

Having worked in my father's funeral home before his passing and my subsequent inheriting the same, I wasn't new to the game of life and death.

Discovering my ability to communicate with spirits, however, was a game-changer. It happened shortly after my 40th birthday and has been a blessing and a curse since then.

The curse was mostly the first terrifying time when I had seen the ghost of a headless man. A demon or some other such ghastly thing took the poor man's head. The details are foggy, but knowing that witches were alive and well in the world and able to battle demons and the like was a relief. It meant I never had to deal with such nonsense in my tiny corner.

The other curse was that I had never seen my father's

ghost, assuming because he passed long before my ability came to light. The rest of the time, my newfound ability was mainly a blessing. It's not a skill you can put on a resume, but it has come in handy more times than I can count.

I pulled into the funeral home's parking lot and saw Radleigh, my friend and mortician, waiting for me by the back entrance. He was wearing a bright pink blazer and a matching bow tie, and his ever-changing short, colored wig for everyday use was a bright purple hue.

Radleigh saved his outlandish, bouffant wigs for his alternate persona—drag queen 'Luna Eclipse.' Radleigh—a mortician by trade—performed as a drag queen on alternate weekends at drag shows in Portland and other cities.

"Morning, sunshine!" he called out in his East Texas accent, waving enthusiastically. I see you've got a new friend with you." Radleigh nodded toward the body bag, scooping Alfie out of his carrier for a good snuggle before letting him go. Alfie ran to the funeral home's door and patiently waited to be let inside.

"Good morning, Radleigh. Yes, this is Mr. Thompson. He passed away at the care home this morning."

Radleigh's face softened, and he offered a sympathetic nod. "Well, we'll take good care of him, won't we, honey?"

Together, we wheeled Mr. Thompson into the preparation room. As we worked, Radleigh filled me in on the latest town gossip, his voice comforting in the otherwise somber atmosphere. When we were finished, Radleigh and I gathered around the small table in the break room. We sipped coffees while reviewing the details of Mr. Thompson's funeral arrangements. I smiled at Radleigh's enthusiasm, even at this early hour. He was a gem, that one.

"Alright, Radleigh," I began, flipping my notebook open and shuffling through the envelope Agnes had given me. "Mr. Thompson has requested a traditional service."

Radleigh flipped open his sparkly pink unicorn-adorned

notebook. "I'll take care of the makeup and dressing," He assured me. "And I've got a new shade of lipstick that will suit him perfectly. 'Cherry Ghost'—it's to die for!"

Radleigh's expertise in theater makeup is unparalleled, thanks to his years as his alternate persona. I trusted him implicitly to ensure Mr. Thompson looked his best for his last farewell.

I laughed at Radleigh's enthusiasm and terrible joke. "Sounds perfect, Radleigh. I know you'll do a wonderful job. Just don't overdo the eye shadow."

Radleigh giggled. "Now, when have you ever known me to overdo anything?"

I slapped the table and snorted. "Never, Rad, not you." I winked. "I'll speak with Reverend Holt about conducting the service. I'm sure he'll be more than happy to oblige."

Radleigh nodded. "I'll ensure the chapel is prepared and fresh flowers are arranged. What about the casket?"

"It looks like Mr. Thompson had chosen the Rosewood model," I replied, consulting his instructions. "If you could place the order, it should be delivered next week."

"Perfect, will do," Radleigh said, his pen scratching across the paper. "I'll make sure it's polished and ready for viewing."

"And we can set the funeral for next Saturday. The Historical Festival starts this weekend, so we need time to manage both. Can you be in attendance? Or do you have a drag show in Lexington or Portland?"

"There are no shows this weekend because of the festival, thankfully." Radleigh swiped his hand across his eyes dramatically. "But I have back-to-back shows after that. I'll write them all on the calendar."

"Thanks, Rad. Perfect."

I shuffled through the remaining papers from Mr. Thompson's package, and among a few loose photos and a tie-clip was a small yellowing envelope.

With *my* name scrawled across it.

In my father's handwriting.

I grasped the envelope, a shiver running through me.

"Carrie? You okay?" Radleigh put down his sparkly pen.

"There's an envelope here. For me. I think it's from my father."

Radleigh got up and came around behind me, placing a warm hand on my shoulder. "Well, don't just sit there like a tumbleweed in a snowstorm. Open it!"

My fingers shook as I opened the small envelope and pulled out a thin, folded paper. Unfolding it, I read one simple sentence.

"Carrigan, if you are reading this, it means I failed, and they got to me. I love you and your mother. I'm sorry. Dad."

CHAPTER 2
SECRETS & SCANDALS

I STOOD UP SUDDENLY, my chair skittering backward, nearly taking Radleigh out. The letter from my father slipped from my clammy hands and floated to the floor.

"Carrigan! What…?" Rad spotted the letter, picked it up, and read it. "What does this mean?"

I paced around the office, my mind ticking a mile a minute. "I'm…not sure, exactly. I mean…I think…"

"Carrie. Sit down for the love of Ru Paul, and tell me what's going on?" Radleigh took my hand and led me to the small sofa. I sat and sighed heavily. Rad held my hand, looking into my eyes expectantly.

"My father. He…died."

"Yes, honey, I know he did. A long time ago, isn't that right?"

"Yes. About…well, over fifteen years ago. A hit-and-run."

Radleigh gasped. "Oh, sweetheart, you never told me that! I mean, I knew he'd died prematurely long before we met, but I just thought perhaps his cholesterol was too high!"

I sniffed out a laugh. "No. He was quite healthy. He was hit by a car when he was away on business in Portland."

"Did they ever catch the guy…?"

I shook my head. "No. Never."

"Well, that's a terrible shame. But if it was a hit-and-run, what's this letter about?"

I took the letter from Radleigh. Rereading it, the heavy burden of grief sat firmly in my belly. "I think it means he was murdered."

"Murdered! Are you sure?"

I got up and started pacing again. "Yes, well, no. Not at all. I've just…had a feeling."

"A feeling? I suppose the authorities didn't agree with your feeling?"

I rolled my eyes and huffed out a breath. "No, not at all. 'A clear case of hit-and-run'. Case closed faster than Blockbuster after Netflix became a thing."

"Oh, honey. That's unfortunate. I hate to say it, but they could be right." Radleigh spoke gently.

I nodded my head. "I know, I know. But this letter—"

"Tells a different story. *Potentially.* Let's not let our imaginations run wild."

I grabbed a thumbtack from the bulletin board beside my desk and tacked the letter. "True. But…"

"Have you ever talked to your dad? You know…his ghost?" Radleigh asked.

I shook my head. "No. My abilities came in long after Dad passed. I sure wish I could talk to him now."

"That's too bad, honey. But…if I could put my friend hat on here…perhaps it's best to let the past stay in the past. At least for now?"

I nodded, sitting at the table and pulling my notebook toward me. "Agreed. There's not much I can do about it now. Let's get back to it, Rad." I smiled. "Thanks for listening."

"Anytime, sugar. Anytime."

———

After finalizing Mr. Thompson's funeral arrangements, we focused on the upcoming annual Historical Festival. As the organizer for this popular event, I took pride in showcasing Castle Point's rich history.

As we chatted, the door to the back room swung open, and Morgana Critt—my mother and reason for needing therapy—swept in. Her high heels clicked against the tile floor. They sounded like a swarm of cicadas coming in for the kill—and caused a literal sweat of dread to fall down my back.

She was dressed impeccably, as always, in a tailored light blue day suit and a string of pearls. "Carrigan, darling," she said, her voice dripping with saccharine sweetness. "I was just passing by and thought I'd pop in to see how you're doing."

I forced a smile, bracing myself for whatever criticism or unsolicited advice she would offer. "Hi, Mother. We are just preparing for the festi—"

"Such fun!" she said, cutting me off.

She looked me up and down disapprovingly over my simple black outfit and cardigan. "Carrigan, must you always dress so... frumpy? You're a funeral director, not a mourner."

I resisted the urge to roll my eyes. "I'm dressed appropriately for the job, Mother. And besides, it's not like I'm trying to impress anyone."

Mother's eyes twinkled mischievously. "Well, that has to change. I've arranged for you to go on a date with a lovely young man I met last week at the country club. He's a lawyer from Portland who's just come to town for the festival and to visit his mother. His name is Julian Ravenscroft, and he's absolutely to die for! I think you two would hit it off splendidly."

Mother's ongoing desire to marry me off to any man with a pulse never ended. "Mother, don't..."

She waved a dismissive hand. "Oh, don't be so dramatic,

Carrigan. It's just a little dinner. You could use a break from all this death and gloom, don't you think?"

I exchanged a helpless look with Radleigh, who was trying his best to suppress a grin. "Mother, I appreciate the thought, but I'm not interested in dating right now. I've got too much on my plate with work. The Historical Festival opens Friday evening!"

Mother sighed, shaking her head. "You're always so focused on your work, Carrigan. Don't you ever think about your personal life? You aren't getting any younger!"

I took a deep breath and counted down from ten in my head, trying to keep my temper in check. "Of course I do. But right now, my work is my priority. And besides, I'm perfectly happy being single." My eyes flitted to the floor, hoping to hide the tiny lie.

Mother looked unconvinced but succumbed. "Fine, have it your way. But don't say I didn't try."

Mom spun on her tiny heel. As she did so, I glanced away, trying to hide my frustration, when my eyes locked with the letter from Dad tacked to the bulletin board. "Mother! Wait." I pulled the letter from its place and showed it to her. "I found this in Mr. Thompson's effects. It's from Dad."

Mother snatched the letter from my hand and read it. Her eyes narrowed. A look I couldn't quite pin down flitted across her face. "What of it?"

I was gobsmacked. "What of it? Mother, doesn't this seem…suspicious to you?"

She waved it away. "Your father and old Thompson were always up to something. Pranksters. It's a joke. Nothing more."

"Mother," I struggled to keep my voice steady, "what if Dad's accident wasn't an accident?"

Mother tossed her head back and laughed. "Don't be ridiculous! Your father was struck down by an idiotic driver–

probably drunk–end of story. Why must you dredge this all up now? Have you no sympathy for my poor nerves?"

I peered at Radleigh, who rolled his eyes. "Sorry, Mother, forget I mentioned it. Have a lovely day. And no more fix-ups!"

With a final air kiss, she turned on her heel and exited the room, leaving a waft of heady perfume and me to wonder if I could ever convince her I was content with my life just the way it was.

Sort-of.

I mean, a boyfriend *would* be lovely. But I had Alfie. And my friends.

Radleigh gave me a sympathetic pat on the shoulder. "Don't worry, Carrigan. Your Mom means well. She wants to forget the past as much as she wants you to be happy."

I sighed, running a hand through my hair. "I know she does. But sometimes, I wish Mother would talk about my father more instead of sweeping his life under the rug, as much as I wished she would accept me for the mastodon I am!"

Radleigh nodded and held up a hand. "Preach, sista! And, if it helps, I wish I had your height and stature. Finding gowns for my drag show would be so much easier! Now, let's focus on making this festival the best one yet. We've got a lot of work and little time to do it."

I forced a smile, grateful for Radleigh's support. He was more than just an employee; he was a genuine friend. "You're right. Let's get back to it."

We reviewed the festival logistics for the next few hours, ensuring everything was covered. Every detail, from vendor booths to food trucks, was too important to overlook.

"Alright, Radleigh," I said, closing my notebook and standing up, towering over my gorgeous man-friend. "I think we've got everything covered. Let's get to it!"

Radleigh stood beside me, a petite frame shadowed by

mine. He beamed at me, his eyes sparkling with excitement. "You can count on it, darlin'. It's going to be a week to remember!"

"I'm heading out for lunch with Trix. Would you like me to grab you something?"

"Oh, yes, please! A Monty Cristo. In the flesh, if you can find him." Radleigh tittered.

"I can manage the sandwich, Rad, not the man," I replied dryly as I headed out the door to the café.

———

The familiar jingle of the bell on the door announced my arrival at the Chatterbox Cafe. The cozy interior, with its checkered tile floor and vintage decor, always made me feel right at home.

Eunice, town gossip and owner of the Chatterbox appeared at my side, a steaming mug of coffee in hand.

"The usual?" she asked, her bright blue eyes sparkling with mischief. Sunlight gleamed off her bold red bouffant hairdo. I squinted down at her.

"You know me too well," I replied, gratefully accepting the mug.

My best friend Trixie spotted me from the seating area and waved enthusiastically. "Carrigan! Over here!" she called out, gesturing to an empty table by the window.

Trixie, a mad crafter and crochet enthusiast, owned The Crafty Cauldron, the local arts and crafts store. She taught me and Radleigh how to crochet, which 'hooked' us, so now we have regular crochet sessions together, calling our little band of merry crafters 'The Hookers.'

I never tire of a good bit of wordplay.

Trixie settled into the chair across from me, her blonde hair brushing the top of her shoulders in loose waves. She wore her signature floral leggings and un-matched top adorned with tiny hummingbirds. A crochet hook resting on one ear jutted out from her hair. I leaned over, snatched it, and handed it to her. She smiled, wrapped her hair up into a small bun, and secured the hook through the bun, holding it in place.

"So, what's new with the 'Corpse Collector'?" she asked, sipping her herbal tea and crocheting. Trixie never went anywhere without a crochet project, multiple balls of yarn, and hooks on hand.

I pulled my crochet project from my bag—a rainbow scarf for Radleigh—and started stitching. "Honestly, it's been a pretty quiet day so far. I just picked up Mr. Thompson from the care home this morning."

Trixie's expression turned serious for a moment. "Oh, I'm so sorry to hear that. He was such a sweet man."

"He was," I agreed, sipping my coffee. "But at least I can help him find peace in the afterlife."

Trixie nodded, her eyes filled with understanding. She and Radleigh were two of the few people in town who knew about my unique ability.

"Speaking of the afterlife," I said, lowering my voice to a conspiratorial whisper, "there was a letter addressed to me in Mr. Thompson's personal effects. From my father."

Trixie leaned forward, her eyes wide with excitement. "Really? What did it say?"

I told Trix about the letter and my thoughts on the subject.

Trixie gave me a small smile and patted my hand. "I know it seems fishy, but let's not jump to any foregone conclusions, okay?"

"That's what Radleigh said, too."

"Well, good advice. No need to worry about something that might mean nothing." Trixie said as she slid a few more stitches into place.

Eunice bustled over to our table with a knowing smile. "So, have you two heard about the latest supernatural happenings at the lighthouse?" she said. Eunice wore hearing aids, finely tuned to any bit of gossip. Her eyes twinkled with amusement.

Trixie and I exchanged a guilty glance before bursting into laughter.

"I have to admit, I'm not surprised," I said, wiping a tear from my eye. "Dealing with the supernatural is part of my daily routine, Eunice." Castle Point was full of supernatural occurrences. In a town where witches were real and ghosts existed, Eunice's "gossip" didn't faze me.

Few residents could communicate with the departed, so I took comfort in knowing I was one of that select group, another of which was my therapist, Alexandra Heale. She wore many hats: therapist, witch, apothecary owner, and wife of our illustrious sheriff, Blake Sheraton, also a witch. I admired their relationship and secretly hoped that I would find someone with as much in common with me as those two.

No matter how common the 'seeing ghost' ability was, I kept mine to myself, as not everyone viewed it as 'normal.' Especially not my Mother. When I tried to share the news of my newfound abilities with her, she shrugged it off with such apparent disbelief that I hadn't bothered to bring it up with her again.

Eunice chuckled, shaking her head. "I heard the ghost of Captain Morgan himself appeared there."

I laughed. "Really. What was he searching for? His missing bottle of rum?" My laughter turned infectious as Trixie joined in on the fun.

"Oh, you two..." Eunice laughed before returning to the counter, her chunky bracelets jangling on her wrists.

Trixie leaned in, her eyes gleaming with tears from laughing too hard. "Hey, do you want to check out the lighthouse tonight? Maybe we'll glimpse Captain Morgan's ghost!"

I raised an eyebrow, a smile playing at the corners of my mouth. "Perhaps help him drink his rum?"

Trixie shrugged, a mischievous grin spread across her face. "Why not? It could be fun!"

I momentarily considered her proposal: "I'm afraid I can't tonight. The Historical Festival starts tomorrow, and there's still much to do."

Trixie's eyes lit up. "I can't wait! We can cruise the lighthouse another time."

Eunice rejoined our table with a fresh pot of coffee and sat beside Trixie. We continued our lively conversation, highlighting the festival. Eunice was in charge of the food vendor trucks, and Trixie was head of the entertainment committee.

I couldn't help but feel grateful for the friendship and camaraderie that came with living in a small town. Sure, it had its share of supernatural undercurrents, but the people made it special.

CHAPTER 3
FESTIVAL & FOLLY

THE FESTIVAL GROUNDS burst into life as I stepped through the wrought-iron gates, the scents of cotton candy and fried dough battling for dominance in the crisp fall air. Strings of lights crisscrossed above, casting a warm glow on the faces below, each one lit up with that special joy that only a community event can brew.

Alfie meowed happily from his carrier on my back. The little gremlin had conned his way into coming with. I don't know why I bothered fighting it. He clearly wears the pants in our household. I was already labeled the 'Corpse Collector.' Why not add 'Crazy Cat Lady' to the list?

Children dashed past, their laughter rising like bubbles. Some stopped to wave at Alfie as parents trailed behind with a watchful eye and indulgent smiles. Artisans lined the walkways, their tables a kaleidoscope of Castle Point's creativity—hand-knitted scarves in every shade, pottery glazed like the ocean at dawn, and paintings that captured our town's unique charm. Local witches manned their booths festooned with potions to cure every ailment, from asthma to warts, intermingled with psychics and tarot readers, all representing the other-worldly aspect of our town.

The rhythmic beat of live music beckoned me toward the center of the festival, where a makeshift stage hosted a local band. Their folk tunes were familiar—comfort food for the soul that had everyone tapping their feet.

I spotted Trixie near the front, swaying to the music with a dancer's grace. Her multicolored crocheted skirt swirled around her like petals in the wind, drawing eyes and smiles from those around her. She caught sight of me and waved exuberantly.

"Carrigan! Come dance!" she called out over the music.

"Two left feet are part of my mastodon charm, but why not?" I placed Alfie's carrier on the grass beside my tote bag and pony-pranced—finger-guns at my hips—toward her as though in a cowboy western. I dropped the 'guns' and grabbed Trixie, spinning her around and around, her skirt flying in all directions, exposing her literal bloomers beneath before spinning her off toward the band, saluting and taking leave.

She laughed and waved, turning back to let the music move her in ways I could only dream of. Collecting Alfie, who was now sleeping soundly at the bottom of his carrier, I was drawn to a quieter corner where an elderly couple sat sharing a funnel cake, their heads close together as they spoke in hushed tones.

A warm feeling settled over me as I watched them—my life might be full of ghosts, but these moments among the living haunted my heart.

A sense of duty nudged me away from the couple's sweet scene, reminding me of my role. I had donned my Event Organizer hat—a felt number with a wide brim that shaded my eyes and, I liked to think, lent me an air of authority and mystery as I walked to the organizer's tent.

Radleigh stood out even in a crowd—the man whose personality seemed too large for his body. His colorful attire, a bright orange suit with a fall-colored floral spray at his lapel and his wig—today an ombre tone—was always matched by an even brighter smile.

"Radleigh!" I called out as he organized a stack of chairs into neat rows.

"Carrigan! Darlin'!" He spun around with theatrical flair before enveloping me in an embrace that smelled faintly of sandalwood and hairspray.

Once he released me from his grip, I asked him, "Are you managing all the set-up tasks, okay?"

"On it like glitter on lip gloss," he quipped.

"Excellent. I will visit some booths and check on our vendors."

"Check away, oh Cap-i-tan." Radleigh bowed dramatically.

I laughed and tugged a clipboard from my tote. Its pages were brimming with layouts and lists, each vendor's name a familiar friend. My first stop was Marcia Well's booth. Marcia and her assistant, Liz, were from Portland and were one of the many out-of-town vendors taking advantage of the well-attended festival.

Her booth was a treasure trove of her cosmetic line, "Trend Savvy." Keeping with the historical theme, she also included a glass case hosting vintage cosmetics that promised a journey back in time. An overhead banner boasted "Beauty Through the Ages," and I was curious.

Pausing before her exhibit, I asked, "Everything okay here?" as I dodged an overenthusiastic toddler hopped up on cotton candy. I perused her range of vintage cosmetics in the display case: glass bottles with ornate labels, powder puffs as soft as whispers, and lipsticks in shades that highlighted the style in decades past. The booth was a patchwork of eras, each a snapshot of bygone beauty standards.

"Quite something, isn't it?" Marcia's voice cut through my reverie.

I turned to find her behind me, her smart navy suit and

sharp features softened by a genuine smile. "It's fascinating," I admitted. "These little pieces must tell some vivid stories."

She nodded, "Oh, indeed. But some things don't change —the lengths we go for beauty." Her gaze shifted to a small vial with a skull and crossbones etched onto its surface, set inside a locked display of antique lipstick tubes and compacts.

My eyebrows rose as I leaned closer. "Poison?"

"Arsenic," she confirmed with a wry grin. "It was used in cosmetics to flush the skin by raising the capillaries to the surface. It was all the rage until people realized it was harming them."

"A deadly beauty," I mused aloud.

"Literally." Marcia's tone was light but carried an edge of criticism toward the reckless vanity of our ancestors.

Alfie started growling low and deep from his backpack behind me, which caused Marcia to give me a puzzling look.

"I'm afraid I'm your worst customer," I admitted, as I wiggled, hoping to calm Alfie down, but only made myself look like a writhing lunatic. "I don't wear a stitch of makeup. Never have."

"You have natural beauty." Liz, Marcia's head cosmetic chemist, joined us. She was dressed as smartly as Marcia, with her almond-brown suit and equally sharp features. Her long, dark hair was a match for Marcia's as well. Both women wore their locks pulled back into a severe bun, secured with crystal and pearl-studded barrettes that glinted in the sunlight.

"Thank you, Liz, although my mother wouldn't agree." I rolled my eyes.

My interest was piqued by the vintage hair permanent products labeled with promises of 'eternal curls' and 'unyielding hold.' These were products that my straight, flat hair could benefit from.

Although the last time I had a permanent, I looked like a

frizzy-haired show dog for the criminally insane for six to eight weeks until it wore off. My mother was mortified.

Liz's laughter rang clear as she picked up a small tin canister. "Hair removal cream from the '40s—supposed to leave you smooth and flawless." She paused for effect. "Except it often left you hairless and red as a lobster."

I winced in sympathetic pain. "That's one way to stand out at a party."

"Indeed." Liz shook her head with mirth twinkling in her eyes.

My gaze traveled over more relics—an eyelash curler that seemed more suited for medieval punishment than beauty enhancement and perfume bottles that smelled like a cross between vinegar and my mother's flower garden.

"The pursuit of beauty has always been a bit... toxic," I said, thinking aloud.

Marcia leaned against her table, her posture relaxed, but her eyes were sharp as ever. "True—historically, at least. And then there's this." She held up a bottle filled with murky liquid—its label faded but still legible: 'Radiant Radium Cream.'

My stomach turned at the thought. "Radium? As in radioactive?"

"The same." Marcia replaced the bottle carefully. "Promised to rejuvenate skin; instead, it..." She trailed off but didn't need to finish—the implications were clear.

"A glowing complexion had a whole new meaning," I said dryly.

Marcia chuckled. "Beauty standards are mirrors reflecting our fears and desires—sometimes dangerous or absurd." She waved her hand across her collection, which included beautiful, gold-sculpted lipstick tubes. "It's all here—the good, bad, and outright ridiculous."

A gaggle of teen girls and their Mother Hen approached their curious expressions, drawing them toward Marcia's booth like moths to a flame. Marcia and Liz seamlessly entered sales mode as I left unnoticed; there were still many booths to visit before the afternoon turned into evening.

My stomach growled, reminding me I'd missed my mid-afternoon snack and the dinner bell was fast approaching. Alfie's howl from the carrier marked his agreement.

Wandering past the patchwork food trucks, I marveled at the cornucopia of scents and sights they offered. A food truck buffet of seafood delicacies harked back to our fishing village days, and more recent imports mirrored the diversity of our little town's growing population.

Eunice Pembleton, the unofficial queen of Castle Point's palates and gossip, stood at the helm of this culinary fleet. She was surveying her kingdom, a clipboard in one hand and a steaming cup of something aromatic in the other. Her red hair seemed to have its own life, defiantly vibrant against the gray sky that promised an evening chill.

"Eunice," I called out as I approached, my breath forming small clouds in the cool evening air.

She turned with a smile that could outshine any light-house beacon. "Carrigan! Isn't this just splendid?" Her eyes swept over her well-orchestrated arrangement of food trucks with pride. Eunice wore her usual bouffant hairdo, overdone makeup, a loud dress, and a string of large blue plastic beads around her neck. She was always a sight that defied convention and a personality to match.

"It's incredible," I agreed, my stomach seconding with an enthusiastic growl. "You've outdone yourself." I unzipped Alfie's backpack and pulled him out, opened a can of cat food, and watched as he scarfed it down.

Eunice chuckled, her gaze fond but calculating as always when she took in the goings-on around her. "Well, it's not just about feeding bodies; it's about feeding souls—with a side of juicy tidbits I pick up along the way."

That piqued my interest as surely as any ghostly whisper

might. "Oh? And what might today's menu include in terms of news?"

Her grin broadened as she leaned closer, conspiratorial. "Well," she began in a hushed tone—however, her voice still carried enough to ensure we would be overheard by anyone who wasn't meant to hear—such are the devious ways of the gossip monger. "You didn't hear it from me, but Marcia Wells is planning to expand her Trend Savvy line—thinks she'll take over the cosmetic world with some kind of exclusive botanical line."

My eyebrows shot up; Marcia was ambitious, but this seemed like quite the leap. "Exclusive? How so?"

Eunice shrugged nonchalantly, though her eyes sparkled with mischief. "Something about a revolutionary botanical skincare range. Claims it'll change beauty as we know it." She paused for dramatic effect. "Of course, Lydia Grant already has something similar..."

"That's... interesting," I said slowly, digesting this new morsel of information.

Eunice wasn't done yet. "And speaking of Lydia," she continued, her voice dropping even lower. "I heard she and Marcia had a row last evening when setting up their tables. Radleigh had to move them apart!"

Lydia Grant moved to Castle Point from Portland last year to open a shop here. She was Marcia's direct competitor, even though Lydia's products boasted using natural ingredients. Her belief in using products derived from nature made her judgmental of anyone who didn't share that belief—Marcia being one of them.

From Eunice's bit of gossip, it would appear that Marcia planned to take her share of the botanical product market. Being as cutthroat as it was, the cosmetic industry likely created quite a rift between the two ladies who were annual festival attendees.

Eunice's tidbit about Lydia and Marcia clashed like

cymbals in my mind. The thought of Radleigh playing peacemaker between two feuding beauty queens brought a smirk to my lips. I'd have to thank him for sparing me that drama.

"I appreciate the intel, Eunice," I said, tucking the nugget of gossip away for later.

She winked, silently acknowledging our shared understanding that information was as much a currency in this town as the dollar bills exchanged at the festival booths.

The surrounding air filled with the sizzle and pop from one truck as someone flipped burgers—a sound that momentarily brought us back to the present festivities and my growling stomach.

Leaving Eunice to her realm, I scooped up Alfie, snagged a burger from one vendor, and navigated through clusters of festival-goers toward the management booth to chat with Radleigh.

"Radleigh!" I called out as I approached. His head whipped around, his ombre wig color catching the light.

"Carrigan!"

I let Alfie out of his carrier to roam the booth. "Eunice filled me in on your heroics around Marcia and Lydia's fight."

He waved a hand dismissively, though his chest puffed out with pride. "Oh, it was nothing. Squabbling over booth placement or some such thing." He leaned in closer, lowering his voice to a playful whisper. "But between you and me, there's enough bad blood between those two to warrant an entire season of soap operas."

I shook my head, amused by his theatrics. "Well, keep me posted if anything else happens."

"You'll be the first to know," he winked.

We chatted while I finished my burger before my responsibilities tugged me away from Radleigh's magnetic pull. I left Alfie in Radleigh's care and headed to Lydia Grant's booth. Knowing her conflict with Marcia Wells made me tread more carefully as I approached.

"Carrigan!" The voice came from behind me—a woman who'd approached without my noticing.

I turned to find my mother sweeping toward me like royalty, gracing her subjects with her presence and reminding me to make an appointment with my therapist, Alexandra.

She was dressed impeccably, as always. Today's choice was a hat that could have served double duty at any Derby Day event.

"Mother," I groaned.

Mother's arched brow spoke volumes without uttering another word. "Carrigan, there you are! I've been looking all over for you."

"I've been making rounds. I was just about to..." I explained hastily before she could launch into one of her lectures about being more 'visible' at events like this one.

"Such fun!" She waved off my words with an elegant flick of her wrist, adorned by one too many bracelets jangling together in harmonious discordance.

"Well," she began, looping her arm through mine with proprietary grace, "you must join me at Mrs. Alcott's booth— she has the most divine hats this year."

My mouth opened to protest—to remind her that duty called—but Mother had never been one to take 'no' for an answer without putting up quite the fight.

"Just for a moment," she coaxed, tugging gently but firmly on my arm.

With an obvious sigh, I allowed myself to be led away by the grand dame of Castle Point society, whose primary hobby seemed to steer my life as one might navigate through treach- erous waters with determination and no small amount of flair.

As we walked arm-in-arm toward Mrs. Alcott's booth— the hat emporium Mother so adored—I prepared myself for the inevitable array of chapeaus she would insist on trying on my head while offering unsolicited advice on everything from fashion choices to personal life decisions, a Critt family tradi-tion as enduring as any other.

Mother examined an ostentatious fascinator adorned with peacock feathers before turning to me, forcing my head down, throwing off my felt hat, and clipping the fascinator onto my head.

"Mother! Ouch!"

"Oh, you look fabulous. See?" she shoved a hand mirror in my direction.

I peered at the image in the mirror, the peacock feathers in the fascinator bobbing about. "I look as though I'm about to take flight. Hard pass, Mother." I yanked the fascinator from my head, pulling out precious strands of my thinning hair in the process.

Standing beside the feathered hats and my mother's hopeful gaze, I gently set the fascinator down. "Another time," I said, offering her a compromising smile before excusing myself from Mrs. Alcott's haven of millinery marvels.

As I weaved back through the crowds toward Lydia's booth, I noticed it was conspicuously unmanned. Her powder puffs and rouge pots sat untouched under a protective sheet.

A tingle of concern pricked at the back of my mind as I searched above the crowd for any sign of her.

Lydia was nowhere to be seen.

CHAPTER 4
DEADLY BEAUTY

I CAUGHT sight of Marcia Wells, her cosmetic booth buzzing with activity close to Lydia's quiet display. She hawked her wares with the zeal of a carnival barker, drawing in a gaggle of eager customers.

"Marcia," I called out as I approached her booth. "Have you seen Lydia today?"

She paused mid-pitch, eyes narrowing slightly as she registered my presence. "Carrigan," she said with a syrupy sweetness that failed to mask her annoyance. "Why would I keep tabs on Lydia? I'm busy enough running my business to give a damn about *hers.*"

Her snark hung in the air like an unwelcome perfume as she turned back to her customers. I muttered a thank you that went unheard—or ignored—and backed away from the booth.

Something felt off. I fished out my phone and dialed Lydia's cell. It rang and rang before I received an indifferent voicemail response. I tried her shop number next. No answer.

Sighing, I slipped the phone back into my pocket, collected Alfie and my bicycle, and pedaled madly to Lydia's cosmetic shop on Main Street. The shop was closer to the festival than Lydia's home, which she shared with her husband, Robert. I'd check with Robert next if she wasn't at the shop.

There were no lights on, inside or out. I pushed the front door, expecting it to be locked, and was surprised it wasn't. The bell above the door announced my arrival into an empty shop filled with silence.

"Lydia?" The name escaped me as a whisper

No reply.

The quaint interior seemed in order—shelves stocked with beautifully labeled jars and bottles, all boasting natural ingredients. Alfie howled, so I let him out of his carrier. He immediately ran toward the counter and howled again.

"Alfie, what's the—"

Lydia Grant lay on the polished wooden floor behind the counter, still as the glass vials around her.

"Lydia!" I yelled, though, judging from her pallor, I knew she wouldn't answer.

I crouched beside her, searching for any sign of life—a breath or a flutter beneath closed eyelids—but nothing. My fingers found her wrist, hoping for a pulse. It wasn't there. I kneeled there momentarily, the world narrowing to Lydia Grant's still form. My heart drummed a frantic beat, drowning out the distant laughter and music of the festival.

The shock of finding her, Lydia, with whom I'd shared countless cups of tea, sent a chill through me. I forced myself to breathe, to focus on what lay before me. Rays of morning sunlight streamed through the shop window and fell across Lydia's face, her skin pale against the dark wood floor. Her short brown hair framed her face in a messy halo from her fall —or possibly from being struck. My gaze swept the surroundings. On the counter above her lay an open book on botanical extracts and a dainty teacup and saucer with remnants of herbal tea leaves dotting the inside.

Alfie was swatting at something shiny near Lydia's body. He continued to bat at it until it came into view.

I gasped.

A lipstick tube lay beside her outstretched hand, its cap off as if it had just been used. I glanced at Lydia's lips. The color in the tube and her lips appeared to be a match—a vibrant red that certainly wouldn't have been Lydia's choice. But the lipstick wasn't one of Lydia's creations—I was sure of that. I recognized the vibrant art déco design from Marcia's booth, the vintage line she boasted about just that morning.

My fingers itched to pick up the tube for closer inspection, but I resisted. Contaminating a potential crime scene was out of the question.

I stood up carefully. Trembling, I pulled out my phone and dialed 911.

"Castle Point Emergency Services, what's your emergency?"

"There's been... there's been a death," I said, my voice steadier than I felt. "Lydia Grant. At her shop on Main Street." I provided the operator with the details. The operator assured me help was on the way and advised me not to touch anything or leave until officers arrived. I agreed mechanically and ended the call.

I looked over the room again, committing every detail to memory: the slight smear of lipstick on her bottom lip that seemed too bright against her pallor, the scattering of papers on her desk suggesting haste or struggle.

As I waited for sirens that seemed to take an eternity, my mind raced with questions. Why would Lydia use one of Marcia's vintage lipsticks? They were competitors in business and philosophy—Lydia's dedication to natural ingredients clashed sharply with Marcia's embrace of modern marketing and vintage allure. The realization hit me like an icy wave: Could it be laced with poison? As Marcia confirmed, arsenic was once a common ingredient in such products. The thought twisted my stomach into knots.

I stood there, feeling a little like the wallpaper—present but fading into the background—as the local authorities arrived and shuffled in and out of Lydia's shop. The hum of their procedural chatter and the crackle of radio static filled the air, which seemed to have thickened with tension since I made the call.

The bell over the door jingled, heralding another arrival. I turned and found myself face-to-face with Deputy Charlie Best. I'd heard about the new deputy in town–sure, a small town—but we'd never met.

Nobody mentioned he was... well, his looks could stop traffic on Main Street—and not in a 'great googlies, look at that terrifying ogre' kind of way.

No, siree Bob. He was tall–taller than me, much to my delight. His features were rugged—the kind that made you think of old-school cowboys—minus the ten-gallon hat. His hair was a shade of brown that sunlight loved to dance in, and his lean build hinted at weekends spent hiking or chopping wood. But his eyes—sharp, assessing, a deep shade of amber—were filled with a profound intellect, reminding you he wasn't just a pretty face.

"Deputy Best," one officer called out, nodding towards me. "This is Carrigan Critt. She found the body."

Charlie approached with a box of donuts and a tray of coffee cups. "Miss Critt," he said in a voice that was both authoritative and gentle. "I'm sorry for this ordeal."

He offered me a small, sympathetic smile that sent my pulse into an embarrassing flutter. I looked up at him—not ignorant of the fact that I had to tilt my head upward to meet his gaze--then reached with a shaky hand to take one of the coffee cups, trying to seem unaffected by his rugged charm.

"Thank you, Deputy Best." I squeaked out, aiming for

composure but landing somewhere closer to a clumsy teenager. "Lovely name. You must be the 'best' deputy," I said with a slight smile. "Everyone's 'bestie'. The 'best of the best,' 'bosom best friend' perhaps? No?"

He raised an eyebrow and offered me a donut. "Here. You look like you could use some sugar."

I hesitated, wanting to argue that I was sweet enough, but took one anyway, thinking a bite might steady my nerves—bad idea. My attempt at a casual nibble resulted in an awkward chunk breaking off and lodging in my throat.

Panic set in as I tried to cough it up discreetly—another bad idea. My face must have been quite the shade of purple because Charlie's concern morphed into action as he set down the coffee tray and moved behind me.

"This may be unpleasant," he warned before delivering a firm Heimlich maneuver that sent the rogue chunk of donut flying across the room.

I gasped for air, mortified beyond belief as tears sprang from my eyes—both from choking and sheer embarrassment.

"Are you alright?" Charlie asked, steadying me with hands on my shoulders as I fought to regain dignity.

"Yeah," I croaked out, then cleared my throat. "Yes, thank you."

He handed me a cup of water someone had thoughtfully provided during my ordeal. As I sipped and tried not to look anyone in the eyes, Charlie shifted back into professional mode.

"So, how did you know Ms. Grant?" he asked gently.

I took a deep breath before answering. "She's an acquaintance. You see, I'm the Historical Festival Coordinator. HFC, if you will. 'Carrigan the Historian,' they call me. No, they don't. Nevermind. What was I saying? Oh right, Lydia hadn't shown up at her festival booth today," I explained, keeping my voice steady despite the lingering redness in my cheeks from both choking and embarrassment. "And she wouldn't answer her phone either, so we came to check on her." I nodded toward Alfie, perched atop the counter, his head bobbing up and down and side to side, watching the officers intently.

Charlie nodded as he jotted down notes on a small pad he'd pulled from his pocket.

"And when was the last time you saw her?" His pen paused above the paper, waiting for my response.

"Yesterday," I said. "When she was setting up her booth at the festival grounds."

"Miss Critt, do you know what happened to Ms. Grant?" Charlie asked, pencil poised.

I nodded. "Possibly. Well, a bit of gossip, really. I heard she had an exchange with Marcia Wells yesterday," I continued after a beat, pushing past the lump forming in my throat at recalling Lydia's vitality just 24 hours prior. "It was apparently... heated."

Charlie's brow furrowed slightly—a tiny line appearing between his eyes—and I realized how even that minor detail seemed important to him.

"Heated, how?" He leaned slightly forward, encouraging me to elaborate.

The scent of his musky cologne tickled my nose hairs. I placed a finger beneath my nostrils, attempting to avoid a sneeze while looking intelligent and thoughtful.

"They were arguing about booth placement, apparently. But I believe it was possibly more about their rival cosmetic lines." I remembered Eunice's gossip about their confrontation. "This is all circumstantial, however. I'm relaying what I heard from Eunice Pempleton."

He nodded again as he scribbled notes, filing away every word.

"And this argument happened where?"

"At Lydia's booth when they were setting up," I said.

"Marcia had approached Lydia; they caused a real ruckus. My friend Radleigh had to break them apart."

Charlie closed his notepad with a soft snap and met my gaze squarely. There was an intensity there now. Despite our earlier awkwardness—he was taking every detail seriously.

"Thank you for sharing that," he said solemnly before giving me another brief smile that did funny things to my stomach. "It helps build a picture of what might've happened."

His gaze lingered on mine for a heartbeat before he turned away to continue his investigation. Left standing amidst officers and fluttering crime scene tape, clutching an empty paper cup like some lifeline, I watched him go about his work with quiet efficiency. I couldn't help but wonder if our paths would cross again under less... chokingly pooptacular circumstances.

My heart finally settled into a rhythm that didn't feel like a drum solo, and I could focus on the task. I followed Deputy Best over to where Lydia lay. The sight of her was jarring.

"Deputy," I began, tucking a stray lock of hair behind my ear to regain some semblance of professionalism, "I noticed something that might be important."

Charlie turned to me, his expression open yet cautious. "Go ahead."

"It's the lipstick next to Lydia's hand," I said, pointing discreetly toward the tube on the floor. "It's from Marcia Wells' vintage collection. I can't imagine Lydia using it given their differences and the possibly lethal ingredients."

His gaze followed my gesture, settling on the tube before snapping back to my face. My heart fluttered irritatingly. "Lethal ingredients?"

"Yes, Marcia has a rather impressive cosmetics collection from the flapper era. Many of the cosmetics of that age contained a poison of one sort or another. The lipstick in the tube matches the lipstick on Lydia's lips. Perhaps it's the reason she's..." I couldn't go on.

"That's an interesting observation, Miss Critt." Charlie stepped closer to the body, his eyes narrowing slightly as he studied the scene. I couldn't help but admire how he seemed to shut out everything else around him when he was focusing. He crouched down beside Lydia, careful not to disturb anything around her. His fingers hovered above the lipstick as if he could absorb its secrets through proximity alone. He made a note on his little pad, then stood back up, meeting Alfie's gaze and mine.

"This the deceased's cat?" he asked, pointing to His Majesty.

"He's mine, actually—Alfie's his name. I can credit him with finding the tube of lipstick beside Lydia's body. You may find tiny paw prints on the tube, I'm afraid. I can assure you, he's not the culprit."

"Thanks for clearing that up and for pointing this out," he said with a smile, showing what appeared to be genuine appreciation.

Feeling slightly buoyed by his acknowledgment, I offered, "I'd be happy to help with the investigation in any way I can."

He glanced around at the other officers, who were diligently cataloging evidence and photographing the scene. "I appreciate that," Charlie replied with a polite nod. But we have protocols to follow. We'll handle it from here."

His words were kind but firm, and I felt a small stab of embarrassment for overstepping my bounds. Of course, they had protocols—what was I thinking?

I bit my lip and nodded in understanding. "Of course, Deputy Best. Just let me know if you need help or... anything else." The words tumbled more awkwardly than a seventh grader at a school dance.

Charlie offered another small smile that seemed reserved for me—or maybe it was just dreaming on my part.

"We'll be in touch if we need your...expertise," his smug smile defined the humor he found in my offer. "Right now, I must arrange for body removal once we've completed our evidence collection."

I opened my mouth to tell him I was the one to call, but he raised a finger and turned, moving a few steps away. I closed my mouth and watched as he consulted his notepad for my number and punched it into his phone.

My phone, tucked in my back pocket, started vibrating. I took a deep breath and answered, "Critt Family Memorial Services, Carrigan Critt, resident Corpse Collector speaking."

"What? Oh, yes, It's Deputy Charlie Best. We require your services at...wait..." Charlie turned toward me.

With the phone still perched at my ear, I waved. "You were saying, deputy?" I continued the call, a small smile tugging at the corners of my mouth.

Charlie eyed me. "You?" I nodded. Charlie laughed, hung up, and walked toward me. His laugh jolted my belly, turning my recent hamburger into pudding. The officers working the scene peered at him questioningly. What could be so funny at a crime scene?

Charlie looked at me from the top down, raised an eyebrow, smiled, and returned to his duties. "I've heard the deputies refer to the 'Corpse Collector' before—I had no idea that was you. Interesting moniker." he smiled, melting my insides.

'Tis me, kind sir. Ready for duty." I gave a jazzy salute, then scolded myself silently for being such a klutz around him. Not only had I choked on a donut, but now I was practically throwing myself at the deputy—eager to help with an investigation that he considered clearly outside my purview.

With one last glance at Lydia's body and the bustling officers around her, I stepped outside into the fresh air. The festival sounds seemed distant now, like echoes from another world.

I scooped Alfie up and snugged him into his carrier. Speaking to another officer, I told him I would drop off my cat, pick up my hearse, and stop at the festival to close Lydia's booth before coming back to collect her body.

I couldn't shake off the feeling that there was more to this than met the eye—and that somehow, someway, I was going to find out what it was, even if Deputy Charlie Best thought I should keep my distance.

CHAPTER 5
GHOSTS & GUILLE

THE FESTIVAL BUZZ had settled into a gentle hum in my head, background noise to the cogs churning in my brain as I discreetly packed Lydia's things. Radleigh and Trixie were both joyfully occupied with their festival duties. I didn't want to put a damper on their day by telling them about Lydia. Not yet, anyway.

I had just about finished packing the last box when my phone buzzed against my butt. It was a call to duty. Lydia's body was ready to pick up.

Tucking my phone away, I stacked the packed boxes at the back of Lydia's booth and strode briskly toward where I'd parked the hearse. As I slid into the driver's seat, the weight of what awaited me pressed coldly against my chest. Lydia Grant—passionate, dedicated Lydia—was gone, and it was my job to collect her from her last moments on this earthly plane.

The drive to Lydia's shop was a blur from the tears burning my eyes. Pulling up outside Lydia's shop, I spotted Deputy Best standing sentinel at the entrance, his presence both comforting and commanding. I stepped out of the hearse and approached him, my boots clicking solemnly on the pavement. He nodded in acknowledgment as I approached, his eyes carrying the day's weight.

"Hey, Deputy Best," I greeted him with practiced neutrality.

"Miss Critt." His voice held steady. "Thanks for coming back."

"Oh, think nothing of it, it's…"

I glanced past him into the shop, where Lydia's body lay still and silent. That's when I saw her—Lydia's ghost—hovering just above her lifeless form, confusion etched into her ethereal features. My heart clenched at the sight.

Poor thing. She didn't even realize she was dead.

I turned back to Charlie, trying to maintain my composure as two worlds collided before me - one living, one dead. I had no clue if Charlie believed in the idea of seeing and speaking to ghosts, like several other officers and the Sheriff, who was himself a natural-born witch, did. I wasn't yet ready to put that to the test. "You're all finished collecting evidence? Do you have any idea what happened?"

He shook his head slightly. "We're still piecing it together. I sent one of the other deputies to speak with the next of kin."

"Ah. Robert Grant, Lydia's husband." I nodded.

Behind him, Lydia's spirit shifted restlessly. She lifted her hazy face and looked at me. "Carrigan? What am I doing here? Why can I see my body?" Her voice trembled like a leaf caught in a breeze.

"Uh," I stammered momentarily, my eyes flitting between Charlie and the ghost. Crafting a sentence in my mind first, I carefully asked, "I was hoping you could fill me in on some details," I said, simultaneously directing my question at Charlie and Lydia.

Charlie raised an eyebrow. "Well, you already know what I know. The rest is under investigation."

I listened with one ear tuned to Charlie and another

attuned to Lydia's ghostly inquiries. "Why can't anyone see me?" she asked with panic.

"Just hang tight for a second," I whispered as Charlie stared at me.

"Sorry?" He paused mid-sentence, confusion, knitting his brows together.

I offered a tight smile. "Just talking to myself...you know how it is."

"Do I?" His tone edged toward amusement as he studied me closely.

Lydia floated closer, her spectral hands wringing in distress. "Carrigan! Please! What's happening to me?"

"It's okay, I'm right here," I murmured, giving Charlie a sidelong glance.

He quirked a brow at me. "I know you're right here. I'm also right here..." He cleared his throat awkwardly and resumed speaking about potential leads and witnesses they were looking into.

As Lydia bemoaned her situation, I nodded to her lamentations and Charlie's procedural rundown until my head bobbed like a demented chicken pecking at a rock.

"This is crazy..." Lydia moaned just as Charlie mentioned gathering evidence.

"Yeah, crazy," I agreed aloud without thinking, causing Charlie to stop once more and look at me with what could only be described as mild alarm. "Yeah...crazy case," I added quickly with an awkward chuckle, hoping he'd buy it as a late reaction to his update.

He gave me a sidelong glance but continued. It wasn't the first time someone thought Carrigan Critt had gone off the deep end—I had quite the reputation for eccentricity—but this time, it felt uncomfortably close to home.

Lydia drifted toward us then, her frustration radiating like heat from sun-baked asphalt. "Can't you see me?" she demanded, looking directly at Charlie.

"It's not that simple," I said softly, eyes darting between Charlie and Lydia's disconcerted gaze.

"What isn't?" Charlie responded immediately after my hushed comment, folding his arms across his chest defensively as if bracing against unseen forces—or perhaps just against my perceived lunacy.

"The situation," I clarified quickly with a forced smile. "It's complex."

Lydia began pacing now—a peculiar sight, given she had no feet to pace with—and threw her hands up in exasperation. "What am I supposed to do now?"

I took a deep breath and let it out slowly before answering my visible and invisible companions. "We'll figure it out."

Charlie nodded while Lydia ceased her tirade long enough for me to ask Charlie if there was anything he wanted me to be aware of before moving Lydia's body—as if I didn't already know what needed to be done. He gave me detailed instructions for preserving evidence during transport when suddenly Lydia swirled around us in an angry, ethereal cloud. A shiver raced down my spine as an icy breeze swept through the room despite no open windows.

Charlie stopped talking mid-sentence and shivered visibly. "Where'd that sudden chill come from?" Charlie muttered as he rubbed his arms briskly for warmth.

"Drafty old buildings," I offered with an air of nonchalance. I set about preparing Lydia's body for transport. Charlie helped me load the body into the hearse.

He gave me a small, two-finger salute. "Thank you, Miss Critt."

"Please, call me Carrigan." Or pet, love, dear or sweetums, pudding-pop, honey-butter, lovey-face…

"Right. Thank you, Carrigan."

I sighed. It would have to do.

I turned away from the hearse and glanced back at Lydia's shop. Lydia's ghost was behind the glass of the front window, her soul trapped in the vortex of the place she expired. Her eyes brimmed with confusion and fear, like a caged bird that had just realized it couldn't fly free.

My breath hitched in my throat at the sight of her spectral form. Her hands pressed against the pane, trying to reach through an invisible barrier. Her eyes shimmered with unshed tears that would never fall—a haunting mirror to my own that threatened to spill over. This wasn't how it was supposed to be; spirits mostly moved on after realizing they'd passed. Lydia just looked lost, a sign that her soul wouldn't settle until the matter of her death was resolved. My heart twisted for her—a woman who had poured her soul into her work now stuck between worlds without so much a by-your-leave. And I could do nothing for her, not here, not now.

Charlie called out from behind me, his voice laced with concern and a touch of impatience. "Carrigan? Everything alright?"

I didn't turn around; my eyes were locked with Lydia's, searching for some way to help her understand or find peace. But what could I say? 'Sorry someone murdered you, but hang tight?' It seemed woefully inadequate.

Lydia raised one hand toward me, palm flat against the glass.

A heavy sigh escaped me as I finally acknowledged there was nothing more to be done tonight. Lydia's spirit was bound here for reasons I intended to uncover—but it wouldn't be tonight. Her hazy form slowly faded from view like a mist dissolving under evening light. An icy wave of loneliness washed over me the moment she disappeared completely. It was one thing to see departing souls; it was another entirely to be privy to their confusion and sorrow in death.

"I'd like to assist with the investigation, Charlie."

Charlie raised his adorable brow in my direction and

shook his head. "Leave it up to the investigators. It's not your job, Miss Critt."

Oh, so we were back to that formality again, were we?

"But I can be very helpful. Honestly, Charlie, if you'd give me the cha—"

"Miss Critt, I appreciate your offer, but please let the professionals handle this, okay?"

As Charlie retreated to his cruiser and started up the engine, I climbed into the driver's seat of the hearse and took one last look at Lydia's shop—the window was now just glass and reflections without her haunting presence behind it. I pulled away from the curb with Lydia's body in the back and Charlie's cruiser following behind like a silent guardian against whatever darkness might try to creep into town tonight.

Resolve settled over me. Charlie couldn't see ghosts and didn't want my help.

Someone had to stand at this peculiar crossroads between life and death and dig into the truth about what happened— and it looked like that someone was going to be me.

———

After ensuring Lydia's body was in the capable hands of the morgue's pathologist, Dr. Loomis, I snatched up my phone and texted Trixie and Radleigh: "Hookers Unite! Emergency crochet-a-thon at my place. Bring wine, bring yarn, bring your sleuthing caps."

Trixie's response was lickety-split: "Be there in a jiff with a rainbow of yarn!" Radleigh was just as quick: "Honey, I've got a Merlot that'll make us forget our names. See you soon!"

As the sun dipped below the horizon, casting long shadows across my living room, I arranged the chairs and sofa into a cozy circle. Alfie roamed from one chair to the couch and over to another chair before settling in for the evening.

The doorbell chimed, and in burst Radleigh with his bottle of wine like a knight brandishing his sword. He wore a shimmering purple scarf that clashed gloriously with his autumn ombre hair.

"Darling, I feel the day in my bones—I so needed this!" he announced.

Before I could reply, Trixie waltzed in behind him, her arms wrapped around a basket overflowing with skeins of yarn as vibrant as her spirit.

"I brought enough colors to crochet a scarf around the town twice," she beamed, placing the basket in the center of our circle. Alfie promptly got up from his seat and jumped into the basket, pawing at the yarn before squirming into the pile and closing his eyes.

We settled in, glasses filled with Radleigh's promised forgetfulness potion.

"I've got something to tell you both," I started, my fingers fumbling with a strand of cerulean yarn. "Lydia Grant... she's dead."

Their reactions were immediate—Radleigh's glass paused mid-air; Trixie dropped her hook with a clatter on the wood floor.

"Dead?" Radleigh echoed. "But I just saw her yesterday! She was arguing with Marcia over something. Wait—is that why her booth is cleaned out?"

I nodded. "Yes, I came back to the festival after finding Lydia's body..."

"*You* found Lydia's body?" They asked in unison.

"Yes. She wasn't at her booth today, and when I called her cell, she didn't answer, so I went to her shop to check up on her and..."

"Well, suck me dry and call me dusty—I can hardly believe it!" Radleigh slapped a palm to his cheek.

"Carrigan, what happened? Do you know?" Trixie asked.

I nodded solemnly. "Honestly, I believe she was poisoned —with arsenic."

"Poisoned!" Radleigh gasped, his free hand thrown to his chest, his other almost spilling his wine. "How?"

I took a sip of wine for courage before confessing to the next part. "It has yet to be confirmed, but yes. There was a tube of Marcia's vintage lipstick beside Lydia's body. Marcia had told me arsenic was one of the main ingredients."

Radleigh let out a low whistle. "That's not your everyday lipstick ingredient."

"No," I agreed, feeling a bitter anger rise. "It's not. Oh, also, I saw Lydia's ghost."

Trixie leaned forward, her eyes wide as saucers. "You did? What was she like?"

"Lost," I admitted, twisting the yarn around my fingers as if it could guide me through this maze. "Confused. She didn't understand she was dead."

"That's heart-wrenching," Trixie murmured.

"And the police?" Radleigh prompted with an arched eyebrow.

I huffed out a laugh without humor. "The new deputy— Charlie Best—practically told me to scuttlebutt out of it after I politely offered to help him. Can you believe it?"

Radleigh rolled his eyes so hard they threatened to orbit his skull. "Clearly, he doesn't know you if he thinks you'll scuttlebutt anywhere."

"We're going to investigate anyway, aren't we?" Trixie asked, her voice determined.

My friends' resolve warmed me more than the wine did. We weren't just going to sit around and dilly-dally while Lydia wandered lost between worlds. Solving her murder was the only way Lydia would finally become 'unstuck' from her place of death and find peace, moving to the 'other side.' Determination settled in the wine-filled warmth of my belly.

"Absolutely. But where do we even start?" I asked, finally starting a chain stitch with my yarn.

"With motives," Trixie suggested. "Who would want Lydia out of the way?”

Radleigh swirled his wine thoughtfully before answering. "Marcia had the most to gain from Lydia pushing up daisies —her business rival gone—poof!" He snapped his fingers. “She could rule the botanical cosmetic industry. And they had that fight yesterday. I practically had to pull them apart!"

I raised a brow and gave him a small slap on the hand. "Rad, I'm sure you're exaggerating. But you're right about the rivalry. Is business rivalry enough for murder?" I pondered aloud.

"It could be if there were more at stake than just sales," Trixie added, creating tight stitches with practiced ease.

"Ooh, like secret formulas or trade secrets," Radleigh mused, tapping his lip with a manicured finger.

The room fell silent as we considered the implications; the only sound was the slide of hooks against yarn woven into works of art.

"Then there's Robert Grant." I mused. "I know that he and Lydia were estranged but not divorced, and with no children, he could inherit..."

We looked at each other across our fortress of yarn balls and partially formed crochet projects in wordless agreement.

“Okay. Tomorrow, I’ll start by interviewing Marcia and then Robert Grant.” I addressed them both.

Radleigh raised his glass in salute and declared firmly, "To uncovering truths and untangling lies!"

Trixie followed suit with her glass and added brightly, "And to keeping Carrigan out of Deputy Best's doghouse!"

Glasses clinked as we solidified our pact beneath the cozy glow of lamplight—our little conclave of crochet and crime-solving firmly resolved to weave through Castle Point's web of secrets one stitch at a time.

CHAPTER 6
ESTRANGED & ENVIOUS

THE FOLLOWING DAY, the fall breeze danced through the vibrant leaves, carrying the tang of salt from the harbor. The hum of my bicycle tires echoed along Main Street, punctuated by the rustle of my jacket as I rode to the Historical Festival, Alfie snugly secured in his backpack carrier.

The buzz of anticipation still hummed in the air and resonated deep inside me despite the pall Lydia's death had cast over my day. I had a mission—to confront Marcia Wells and gauge her reaction to the tragic news.

As I threaded through clusters of townsfolk, Marcia's Trend Savvy table came into view. Marcia herself was like a polished gem amidst the rustic setting. Her sharp eyes locked onto mine as I approached, a practiced smile gracing her lips.

"Miss Critt, are you back to try on some of my products?" she teased, though her eyes held an edge.

I returned her smile with a measured one of my own. "Marcia, I've come with some rather grim news."

Her perfectly shaped eyebrow arched in curiosity. "Oh?"

"It's about Lydia Grant." I watched her face closely. "She was found dead yesterday morning."

The color drained from Marcia's face, her facade cracking

momentarily before regaining composure. "Dead? That's... that's shocking." Her voice wavered only slightly.

"Isn't it?" I leaned in, keeping my voice low. "I heard you two had quite the spat while setting up your booths the other day."

Marcia stiffened and glanced toward Lydia's now empty booth. "Lydia and I had our differences, but business is just business."

"And where were you after the setup was complete?"

Her lips pressed into a thin line before she replied. "I had a meeting," she said tersely." And before you ask, yes, people can vouch for that." Her annoyance was palpable. She crossed her arms over her chest and stared me down.

I met her gaze. "It's just routine questioning, Marcia."

"Routine or not, it feels rather pointed. And who are you to be asking, anyway? You're not the police."

"I'm just being helpful."

Marcia exhaled sharply but offered a curt nod. "You'll find nothing here but lipstick and liner, Miss Critt."

With that dismissal, I turned my attention to Marcia's vintage cosmetic display case. The display was meticulous, a curated selection of powders, rouges, and lip colors arranged against a backdrop of black and white photographs depicting women of yesteryear. I could almost hear the swish of petti-coats and the tinkle of laughter as I imagined them preening before their vanities.

The centerpiece was an array of lipsticks, their slender tubes lined up like soldiers on parade. My eyes traced over them, counting the tubes.

Marcia watched me across the table, her eyes sharp as cut glass. I could feel her scrutiny. I straightened up and met her gaze.

"Quite the collection," I called over to her. "Just how many lipsticks are there?"

She approached with measured steps. "They've been a hit

with the festival goers," she replied coolly. "There's twelve in all."

I nodded. "But I count eleven. One appears to be missing."

Her lips tightened as she eyed the collection. "Well, that's strange. Liz?"

"Yes?" Liz pulled away from a small cluster of customers.

"There's a tube missing from the vintage display."

Liz tapped the glass, counting out eleven tubes. "Huh. That's strange. I'm sure there were a dozen here when I set up the display yesterday,"

I tilted my head to one side. "I think I may know where your missing lipstick wound up," I began, my voice casual but my heart hammering against my ribs, "a vintage tube was found beside Lydia Grant's body yesterday morning."

Liz's eyebrows shot up. "Lydia Grant? She's...? Oh, my God."

"Yes, very unfortunate. The police are looking into the possibility that she was poisoned with one of your lipsticks." I watched both women for clues of guilt.

Marcia's composure slipped briefly before she masked it with a scoff. "One of *my* lipsticks, the murder weapon? That's unlikely."

I pushed the point. "Well, as I said, one was found on the scene. Did either of you give it to her?"

Marcia's denial was swift and vehement. "No," she said firmly.

Liz added, "I did not give Lydia any lipstick either."

"So, you sold her one?" I prodded, searching Marcia's eyes.

Her gaze faltered before locking eyes with me again. "No, these items are not for sale. They're my private collection."

"And neither of you can recall anyone taking anything from the display?"

They both shook their heads with exasperated sighs.

"People come and go all day long here," Marcia gestured broadly at the crowds milling around us. "Besides, we keep the display locked unless we show a patron—such as yourself—the contents."

Liz agreed. "Someone must have broken into the display case at night or stolen one when the display was open," she stated flatly.

"Possibly," I conceded with a nod. "However, the festival gates are locked at night. It would have been difficult for anyone to get anywhere near your display after the gates closed," I paused for effect. "Liz, where were you the night after the festival setup?" I asked.

"I was in my hotel room, sleeping."

"Can anyone attest to seeing you there? Did you have any…visitors?"

"I was *alone*," she punctuated the last word. "However, the hotel staff saw me go to my room."

I addressed both the women. "If that lipstick had anything to do with Lydia's death..."

Marcia cut me off with a sharp wave of her hand. "It didn't come from me or Liz," she insisted again.

Her certainty seemed genuine—or at least well-feigned—but there was something in her manner that niggled at me like a splinter under the skin.

"You understand why this is suspicious?" I pressed.

Marcia folded her arms across her chest defensively, her expression steely. "Suspicion isn't evidence," she retorted. "I could have easily been robbed—even by you, Miss Critt."

"True," I conceded with a nod. However, the festival grounds gates are locked at night. It would have been difficult for someone other than you to get anywhere near your display," I paused for effect. "And you are the one with motive, not me."

"*Me? Motive?*" Marcia asked, hand to chest. "I don't know what you're talking about."

"Yes, you. You and Lydia were competitors. Having her out of the way would be rather convenient…"

Marcia scoffed. "Preposterous. My business was more profitable than Lydia's. Ridiculous!"

We stood momentarily in a silent standoff, Marcia and Liz unwavering in their denial and me weighing every angle like pieces in a jigsaw puzzle, refusing to fit together neatly.

"I'm certain the police will want to examine your collection," I said, breaking our impasse.

"They'll look at nothing," Marcia replied tersely, "without a warrant."

———

Now out of his backpack and curled up in the passenger seat of the hearse, Alfie snored softly. He was an unusual boy, as few cats enjoyed car rides. Fewer cats enjoyed backpack carriers or could see ghosts, either. Alfie was indeed an enigma.

I drove to the Grant residence, a charming Victorian that now seemed to loom ominously. Supposedly, Robert Grant and Lydia had been estranged for the past year. Although they kept the same residence, Lydia told close friends they no longer shared a bedroom.

Fortunately, or unfortunately, depending on the point of view, her close friends were part of the gossip network, which Eunice was privy to, so I knew this long before Lydia's demise.

I also knew Robert had received the tragic news from the deputies before my arrival. When he opened the door, his face was etched with grief, making the lines around his eyes appear deeper and more pronounced.

I stepped inside, offering a hand, "Robert, I'm so sorry for your loss."

He glanced at my hand as if it were a foreign object before

shaking it limply. "Thank you," he murmured, his voice strained.

Robert led me to the parlor, a room that, like the rest of the house, must have seen happier times. Sunlight streamed through lace curtains, casting delicate shadows over a collection of antique furniture. The air smelled of lemon polish.

The walls were adorned with portraits, each frame capturing generations of Grants with stern expressions and formal attire. In the center of it all, an oriental rug lay beneath a coffee table laden with magazines about real estate—a modern contrast to the room's historical grandeur.

He motioned to a floral-patterned settee with a hand that seemed heavier than before. "Please, sit."

I perched on the edge, my hands clasped in my lap to still their restlessness. "Robert, I know this must be incredibly hard for you. Lydia was... well, she was one of a kind."

His smile was tight. "That she was."

A flash of white caught my eye as a cockatiel perched atop the bookshelf. I was grateful I'd left Alfie asleep in the hearse, or he'd likely think the bird was his prize. The bird launched itself into the air and landed unceremoniously on my head. Robert didn't seem to notice—or care—as he sank into an armchair and stared at his hands.

"That's quite a friendly bird you've got," I said, forcing a smile while imagining all the places bird droppings could ruin my black sweater.

"Jasper," he said with a faint smile. "He likes company."

Jasper nibbled at a strand of my hair, and I suppressed the urge to duck and cover. Instead, I stayed put, trying to appear unfazed by my new feathery hat.

"Did Lydia ever mention anything unusual leading up to...?" My voice trailed off as Robert's gaze hardened.

"She was always into something or other with her cosmetics—natural this, botanical that," he said dismissively. Jasper flapped his wings and settled more comfortably on my head. I could feel the sharp little pin-pricks of his claws etching into my scalp.

As Robert talked about Lydia's business endeavors with detached curiosity rather than sorrow, Jasper decided my ear looked tasty and gave it a gentle peck.

"Ow! Jasper, no snacks," I scolded under my breath, swatting at him when Robert looked away to retrieve a crumpled tissue from his pocket. The bird squawked indignantly and flew around the room, only to return to his roost atop my head moments later.

Robert dabbed at his eyes with the tissue, his attention fixed on anything but me or his avian companion. "I just can't believe she's gone. The police are saying she was allegedly murdered. Can you believe that?"

"I know this is hard." My words felt hollow as Jasper started an interpretive dance across my scalp. "And you've probably been asked this already, but—"

He cut me off sharply. "Yes, the police thoroughly questioned where I was that night."

"And?"

His eyes flashed with irritation. "At a real estate conference in Portland. Check with anyone there; they'll tell you."

"I'm not doubting you," I assured him quickly, reaching up again as Jasper made another pass at my earlobe. "Just trying to help."

"Wait, a moment. What business is it of yours?" Robert asked, suddenly cold. "Aren't you here to ask about funeral arrangements?"

I met his gaze squarely, ignoring Jasper's antics for the moment. "Yes, of course. I just…"

Robert's face tightened like he'd bitten into something sour, and he cut in. "Look. Lydia wasn't perfect. She had many secrets."

This was news.

The Lydia I knew was an open book. Her gentle demeanor

and amiable nature had earned her the affection of everyone in town. As a businesswoman, she exuded a warmth that drew people to her, making it hard to imagine she could harbor any hidden truths.

"Could one of those secrets have led to her being murdered?" I pressed gently. Jasper finally fled from my head and returned to his perch, high on the bookshelf. I straightened my catawampus hair, mindful of finding any of Jasper's deposits. Thankfully, there were none.

He looked away from me, his eyes scanning the room as if the answer might be written on its walls. "Lydia's passion for her work... it bordered on obsession." He shook his head slowly. "Sure, she had many competitors. What business doesn't? But...murder?"

The silence stretched between us until he finally spoke again.

"Robert, I know this is difficult, but I must ask: did Lydia have any enemies?"

He paused and looked me in the eye. "I suppose her competitors were..." he admitted.

"Can you think of anyone who might benefit from her death?" I watched him closely.

He hesitated before responding. "Benefit? Myself, I guess. I'm her sole heir." A flicker of discomfort crossed his features —subtle but there.

I leaned forward slightly. "Yes, but assuming you aren't Lydia's murderer, do you know anyone else who could have a motive?" I hoped for a clue into Robert's knowledge of a dispute between Marcia Wells and Lydia.

Robert's mouth formed a tight line as he weighed my words.

"Well, just me, I suppose," he said after what felt like an eternity, "there were tensions between us. But I didn't kill her!"

Okay, so no mention of Marcia. Perhaps Lydia didn't

convey her business dealings with Robert since their estrangement. I nodded encouragingly.

"Lydia and I hadn't lived together—as a married couple, that is—for over a year," he continued defensively.

"I'm aware," I said softly, "and you inherit...everything?" He shifted in his seat, clearly uncomfortable with where this conversation was headed. "Robert, you are what the police will call a 'prime suspect.' I assume you aren't in a cell because the police are looking into your alibi."

I watched as his jaw clenched. Robert stood abruptly and walked over to one of the large windows overlooking the gardens—gardens Lydia had once tended to with meticulous care.

"Robert, were you privy to any goings-on between Lydia and Marcia Wells?" I thought being more direct was the only option.

Robert's posture seemed to straighten. "Certainly. They are–were–cosmetic rivals."

"Do you know if Marcia would have taken that rivalry... further?"

Robert turned toward me, eyes wide. "You think Marcia had something to do with Lydia's death?"

"There are potentially two people who would have a reason. Marcia, and...yourself."

"You're right," he conceded. "I had reasons for wanting Lydia out of my life." He paused as if struggling with an internal battle before facing me again. "But not dead."

I released a slow breath I hadn't realized I'd been holding and rose from my seat. "I understand this is difficult--"

"You understand nothing," he cut in sharply.

I stood still momentarily before responding calmly, "Maybe not all of it, Robert. But enough to know when someone's holding back."

His eyes narrowed as if trying to read my thoughts.

"If you think of anything else that might help, you must

tell me–or the police." I handed him my card despite knowing he already had my number; it was a gesture more than anything else. "We can work on the funeral arrangement another time after the police finish their investigation."

Robert took it without looking at it and set it down on the table beside him—a noncommittal response if ever there was one.

As I moved toward the door, I glanced back at him silhouetted against the window light; there was more to Robert Grant than just an estranged husband dealing with grief—of that much, I was sure.

Just as my hand touched the doorknob, Robert spoke again.

"Carrigan?" His voice held something new now; resignation perhaps?

"Yes?" I turned back to face him expectantly.

He sighed deeply before answering. "If it helps... Lydia kept journals—lots of them."

Journals? My interest piqued instantly.

"Where can I find these journals?" My voice betrayed none of the eagerness that surged within me.

"In her office—at the shop." He seemed almost reluctant to share this information with me but must've realized its potential importance.

"Did you tell the police?"

"No, I hadn't thought about it until now." he shook his head solemnly.

"No worries, Robert. I'll take care of it."

"Thank you," I said sincerely. It was precisely the lead I needed—one that might unravel this twisted affair.

Robert merely nodded in acknowledgment as I left the room behind me—a room filled with relics of marriage long since faded.

Robert let out a heavy sigh but said nothing more as he

walked me out. At the door, I turned back toward him. "If there's anything you remember or need..."

He nodded stiffly and closed the door before I could finish.

I exhaled slowly and stepped off the porch. My resolve hardened with each step away from the house; Lydia's story wasn't over yet—not by a long shot.

CHAPTER 7
ARSENIC & ALIBIS

THE NEXT DAY, the festival unfurled under a cobalt sky, banners flapping like the wings of colorful birds eager to take flight. Radleigh, clad in a shirt that matched the morning's vibrancy, was organizing festival maps and schedules. I leaned against the back of our booth, nursing a coffee. The festival buzzed around us, yet my mind was tethered to my conversations with Marcia Wells and Robert Grant. Alfie roamed the booth, settling at my feet as Trixie approached, her smile as wide as the sky.

"Hey Carrigan, hey Rad." We gave her a 'hey' back. Her voice dropped to a whisper. "Any news about...you know..."

I quietly told Radleigh and Trixie about the confrontation with Marcia and Liz and my visit with Robert—leaving out the part about Jasper using my head as a perch—but told them about Lydia's journals.

Radleigh leaned against the cold metal table with a frown. "Both Marcia and Robert have solid motives. Marcia to eliminate the competition, and Robert for the inheritance."

"It seems so, yes." The idea left a bitter taste in my mouth. "But why go to such lengths? Surely they'd know they'd be the prime suspects? We can't eliminate either of them but can't stop there. We need to look closely at her other connections."

"Even someone as nice as Lydia could have a lot of enemies," Radleigh said.

Trixie agreed. "We owe it to Lydia to figure this out. Has Charlie confirmed how she died? Was it the arsenic in the lipstick?" Trixie asked.

"They're testing it now," I answered.

The question that loomed over us was why. Lydia was well-liked in Castle Point. Robert mentioned she had enemies. Who—other than Marcia—were they, and what were they after? I glanced at Radleigh, finding his gaze already on me. "What are you thinking?" I asked.

"I'm thinking Lydia either stumbled on something or possessed something. Something worth killing for,"

Trixie nodded slowly. "That's what we need to find out."

"Let's look for those journals tonight at Lydia's shop. You two in the mood for a little break-and-enter?" I asked in a low whisper.

Radleigh and Trixie grinned excitedly, shared high-fives, then bumped butts.

My phone dinged. My heart sped up as I read Charlie's name.

Charlie: *"Arsenic confirmed. Lydia Grant's death was no accident."*

I texted back, my long fingers fumbling frantically like a toddler hopped up on Coco Puffs: *"Artistry? In her lipo-suction?"*

Damn, autocorrect.

Charlie: *"???"*

Me: *"Sorry, all thumbs today. Arsenic? On the lily pad?"*

DAMMIT!

Me: *"Liposuction,"*

Me: *"LIVERPOOL!"*

Charlie: *"Do you mean 'lipstick'?"*

Me: *"Yes. Yes, I do."*

Charlie: "It's being tested now."

And with that horrifying episode over with, I would see myself to the nearest bridge.

———

The shop's back door creaked, a soft complaint against the silent night. "Excellent work, Radleigh," I whispered, as he successfully worked the lock using a couple of bobby pins that held his wig in place.

He waved, securing the pins back into place at the nape of his neck. "Nothing I can't do with a couple of hairpins."

The back door led directly into Lydia's office. We moved like phantoms through the space. My four-legged shadow, Alfie, padded in behind me, whiskers twitching in the moonlight. Trixie and Radleigh followed, their breaths weaving steamy ribbons into the air. "Okay, darlings," Radleigh whispered, his eyes scanning the dark interior of Lydia's shop. "Let's find the journals and make it snappy."

Trixie nodded. "I'll check the shelves; you guys take the desk."

Alfie let out a tiny meow to remind us he was there for moral support and jumped up on the desk. I pulled open the desk drawers one by one, and a higgledy-piggledy mess of papers and knick-knacks greeted me. "Found them!" I hissed, my fingers brushing against leather-bound spines tucked at the back of the bottom drawer.

Radleigh scooted over, a grin splitting his face as he helped me haul out the trove of secrets. Trixie joined us on the floor, her eyes wide with curiosity.

I flipped open the first journal. "Let's see what Lydia was hiding."

As we leafed through pages filled with meticulous notes

and personal reflections, Alfie curled beside me, purring contentedly despite our illicit endeavor.

Trixie muttered. "She wrote about everyone and everything, but no names, just initials…"

I pointed at a passage with two initials: "MW. Marcia Wells," I murmured. "That one's easy. Also RG. Robert Grant."

"But what's this 'up to no good' about MW and JR?" Radleigh mused aloud. "Who's JR?"

We pondered silently before Trixie suggested, "Maybe it's Julian Ravenscroft? I heard from Eunice that he's her lawyer."

"Could be," I nodded and wrinkled my nose. "He's also the fellow my mother's been trying to set me up with."

The pages rustled as we continued our search until another initial surfaced: VV. One entry read, 'VV won't pay,' and another, on another page, read, 'VV came for a visit.' These entries, and others like them, seemed incongruent—some upsetting, some pleasant.

"I'm flummoxed," I admitted. "Who on earth could this VV be?"

We exchanged puzzled glances.

"I'm not sure," Radleigh offered hesitantly. "In a few of her notes, she refers to VV as if it were two people."

"Exactly," I agreed.

Trixie shrugged. "Could be anyone. Or any two… We could start our search by going through the phone book."

"The phone book? What year are we in, 1955?" Radleigh joked. "Honey, I haven't seen a phone book since 2001 when Elton John won an award at the 43rd Grammy's."

"Gee, Rad. Sorry, I don't measure time on your favorite knighted singer's life events. But okay, point taken. Hey, look at this." Trixie pointed to an entry dated just the week before. It spoke of a suspicion: MW and JR were concocting some clandestine plan to take something from Lydia.

"We need to find out who MW and JR are for certain," I said firmly. "And what they were planning to take."

"Agreed. Sounds suspicious, whatever it is." I said.

The clock ticked mockingly from its perch on the wall, urging us to piece together Lydia's cryptic clues before time—or someone—caught up with us.

A sudden chill brushed past us, and I felt Lydia's presence nearby. Alfie's spine arched, fur standing on end as he hissed into the stillness of Lydia's shop. His reaction caught me off guard; Alfie was usually calm, even in the presence of spirits. I followed his gaze to the corner, where a subtle shift in the light marked her arrival.

Lydia Grant materialized before me, her spectral form wavering like a mirage. She clutched at her chest, eyes wide. Her mouth moved without a sound before a faint whisper finally broke through. "I... I can't believe I'm... Is this real?" Her voice trailed off to a delicate echo.

I tried to ground myself against her sorrow. "Lydia, I know this is overwhelming, but I can help you."

Trixie and Radleigh dropped the journals they were reading and watched in silent understanding.

"Carrigan?" Lydia's voice echoed, confusion etching lines across her brow. "What are you doing with my..." her gaze fell across the pile of opened journals on the floor.

"The journals," I urged gently, tapping the worn leather cover of one lying open on the counter. "You wrote about several people, the initials VV, JR, RG, and MW. We think at least one of them is tied to your death."

Lydia floated closer, peering at her handwriting as if it were foreign. "So angry... they were all so angry..." Her voice faded as she struggled to piece together fragments of memory.

"Lydia, who's MW?" I pressed, watching her closely.

"Marcia Wells," she murmured. "She...stealing—a thief—but...it's mine..." A shadow crossed her face, a mixture of fear and defiance that had likely been mirrored in her life.

"What did she take?" I watched Lydia's expression for any flicker of recognition.

Lydia shook her head, wisps of hair drifting ethereally around her face. "Nothing, but she tried. I don't remember clearly... all so...foggy." She looked up at me with an apologetic gaze that tugged at my heartstrings.

"It's okay," I reassured her, even as frustration gnawed at me. "What about the initials VV? Can you remember who that is? Take your time."

She floated back and forth as if pacing, passing through a display stand without disturbing a bottle. "VV wouldn't pay..." Her hands clenched in an impotent fist.

"Can you remember a name?" My fists tightened around the journal pages.

"No," she whispered with despair. "It's all hazy—like trying to recall a bad dream."

I bit my lip, pondering our next move, when Alfie suddenly pawed at a page in the journal, his claws catching on an entry dated just weeks prior. Lydia leaned in closer, squinting at Alfie's selection. "It's...oh, what's that name...?" she said slowly, tapping her ghostly finger against her temple. "I have something they want. Something they all want..."

"Something they want? What is it?" My pulse quickened.

"They said they would ruin me..." Lydia's form flickered like a candle in a draft.

"What is the something they want?" I pressed further.

Her apparition wavered more intensely as she struggled to hold on to her presence. "It's... slipping away..." The edges of her figure blurred into nothingness just as she whispered something indiscernible.

I leaned forward instinctively, reaching out only to grasp empty air. Lydia was gone, leaving a silence that rang louder than any words. Alfie mewed softly beside me, his green eyes reflecting my disappointment. He jumped off the desk and sauntered from the office into the shop with a meow that broke the silence.

A journal lay open under my fingers. VV—We had initials, but no name, face, or motive—yet. And Marcia Wells. What did Lydia mean by 'stealing thief'? Was blackmail involved? My mind raced with questions that hung unanswered in the ghostly aftermath of Lydia's visitation. I closed Lydia's journal gently, feeling its weight heavy with secrets. A chill crept up my spine—not from any spectral presence but from the realization that Lydia's killer was still out there—breathing our air, walking our streets.

And somewhere in these pages lay the key to unmasking them; we just needed to decipher Lydia's cryptic messages.

We could hear Alfie scuttle across the wooden floorboards in the central part of the store. "What are you up to, Mister Man?" I called out and was immediately answered by a solemn wail and more scuttling.

"Ew, I hope it's not a mouse." Radleigh pulled his legs up onto the chair he was in, his face pinched in disgust.

"Oh, Rad. Scared of a little mouse." Trixie giggled. Radleigh leaned over to give her a light smack against her arm.

Getting up and shaking my sleepy legs, I stepped from the office into the shop. Alfie, paws skittering, claws tapping rapidly as he batted at a shiny fragment nestled between two floorboards. My curiosity piqued, and I crouched beside him, peering at the small object he found so fascinating.

"What have you got there, you little pilferer?" I teased, reaching to retrieve the item before Alfie decided it was his new chew toy.

It was a jagged piece of plastic with a tiny bobble–the size and color of a little pearl–attached. Its sharp edges caught the dim light filtering through the shop's dusty windows. It looked like it could have been part of a barrette or a fancy hair comb, the kind used to hold back a long lock of hair. I turned the fragment over in my hand, thinking of Lydia, remembering her locks to be relatively thick. I surmised it was likely hers.

"Well, this could be a piece of diddly squat or an important clue," I murmured. The little find had added another layer to this brouhaha.

"Did you find something interesting? Was it a mouse?" Radleigh inquired as I stepped back into the office.

"No mouse, no. Possibly a little clue," I replied, showing the piece to Rad and Trix. "Alfie's got a nose for mischief—and maybe evidence."

"It looks like a broken piece of a hair comb," Trixie said as she busied herself making a pot of tea in the shop's tiny kitchen nook. She handed us each a cup, and I took it gratefully, letting the liquid soothe my parched throat and warm my cockles.

"It does, indeed." I agreed.

"Could be nothing but a piece of broken plastic." Radleigh mused aloud before taking a sip of his tea.

"Or it could be something that ties everything together." I couldn't shake off that inkling—the kind that tickles at your brain until you pay it to mind. I shoved the broken piece into my pocket and picked up a journal. "Okay, Hookers. We've got initials to decode and motives to untangle."

"We need to figure out whose initials these are before we can devise a possible motive." Radleigh offered, looking at me over the top of his tiny, bright, fuchsia reading glasses perched on the end of his nose.

I grabbed a stack of paper and several pens from the desk drawer and passed them to my little crew. "Let's copy out as much info as possible from the journals tonight. Tomorrow, I'll turn them over to Deputy Best."

A chorus of agreements filled the room as Alfie strolled back into the office, jumped onto the desk, and made himself comfortable amid our pile of potential evidence.

With every page turned, more questions surfaced like bubbles in a cauldron. Hours later, we gathered the journals scattered across the office floor. Radleigh helped me stack them neatly and tuck them back into the drawer while Trixie tidied the office.

"Time to skedaddle," she announced, "before someone finds us. Hey, look!" She pointed to a key hanging beside the back door. I grabbed it and tried it in the door. It worked. I tucked it into my pocket beside the bit of pearl and plastic.

With Alfie in tow, we exited Lydia's shop, leaving behind Lydia's anguished spirit. As we walked through the cobbled streets toward home, Trixie linked her arm with mine. "So, Miss Critt, do you have any thoughts on Lydia's murderer? Or are you flummoxed?"

"I'm as muddleheaded as my blind 87-year-old aunty looking for yarn in a shoe store," I confessed with a laugh that didn't quite mask my frustration. "But this,"—I patted my pocket where the plastic shard rested—"might just unravel some of this rigmarole."

Radleigh offered an encouraging smile. "Honey, you've got more investigative intuition in your pinky finger than most deputies have in their whole brain." His drawl was comforting.

"I just wish Lydia could've given us more to go on," I sighed. The weight of responsibility pressed on me—this wasn't just about solving a puzzle; it was about justice for a life stolen too soon.

CHAPTER 8

PILFER & PREDICAMENT

AFTER OUR LONG night of note-taking and contemplation, sleep clung to my eyes. As I got ready to leave, Alfie, clearly feeling the effects of the late evening, slowly padded to his kitty backpack and pawed at the zipper.

"You sure? You look exhausted." We both yawned. Alfie forced the case apart with his bulk and jumped inside—a decision made. "Okay, fine. I guess you're coming with." I slipped the carrier on my back and texted Charlie.

Me: *"I have something important to tell you. Can you meet me at Lydia's shop?"*

Charlie: "On my way…"

I rode my bicycle to the shop and waited. A flutter stirred in my chest as Charlie pulled up and strode towards the door, his uniform crisply defining the authority he wore as comfortably as his skin. His aftershave sent my senses into a tailspin.

With formalities out of the way, I leaned closer to Charlie. "We should talk—inside."

He nodded and, taking the master key out of his pocket—confiscated from Lydia's belongings by his deputies during the investigation—unlocked the shop. Releasing Alfie from the confines of his carrier to roam the shop, I took a deep breath. I shared everything about my meeting with Marcia, Liz, and Robert Grant, including the tension between the estranged couple and Robert disclosing Lydia's journals.

Charlie listened intently, his face a mask of professionalism etched with concern. When I finished, he let out a long breath.

"Thank you for bringing this to my attention," he said.

"And you got the results back on the lipstick? Was it arsenic?"

Charlie rubbed his chin, hesitating, then nodded. "Yes, arsenic. But not enough to kill someone. It had to have been administered another way."

Alfie's yowl interrupted us. He was sitting atop the shop counter, pawing at something. I walked over to him. He tapped at a teacup and saucer, remnants of Lydia's last cup of tea growing moldy inside.

"Alfie! Brilliant!"

Charlie joined us at the counter as I scooped Alfie up. "Your deputies missed a vital clue..." I pointed at the cup. "How the arsenic was delivered, I suspect." Head held high. I took my small victory.

Charlie pulled a plastic evidence bag and a pair of latex gloves from the inside pocket of his jacket and placed the teacup and saucer inside without saying a word.

He looked past me toward Lydia's office. "The journals are likely in her office," he said, brushing past me. I followed, letting Alfie return to his snooping.

I watched as Charlie slid open drawer after drawer until he found the journals exactly where I'd returned them.

Charlie reached for the leather-bound volumes, his fingers grazing the pages as he flipped through them. "You said these contain potential leads?" His voice was steady, and his eyes scanned Lydia's meticulous entries for clues.

"Well, I don't know, exactly..." I lied. "Robert just mentioned them as if they'd contain important secrets..." I picked up a journal and flipped it open, reading a line briefly before Charlie snatched it from me.

"Miss Critt, I've told you before, leave the investigating to the investigators…" Charlie huffed.

"I'm sorry, but I know I can be helpful. I know practically everyone in this town, so if Lydia's journals mention some-one…well…I could help," I replied sheepishly. I dare not tell him we had read the journals last night and made copious notes, but I was glad we did.

A chill seeped into the room as he continued to peruse the pages—a sign I knew all too well. Turning slightly, I caught sight of Lydia's ghost hovering near her desk, her spectral eyes wide with urgency.

Lydia's ghost whispered, her voice like wind through fall leaves, "Carrigan... help me."

I nodded subtly to her while maintaining my composure in front of Charlie. I leaned over, reading the open journal upside down. "So, any thoughts on who VV might be?" I asked Lydia aloud, hoping to keep my dual conversation under wraps.

Charlie frowned, pulling the journal from my view. He rubbed his chin thoughtfully. "Too vague to draw any conclu-sions just yet."

Lydia floated closer to Charlie, her transparent hand reaching his shoulder as if she wanted to shake him into awareness. I winced at her proximity to him, bit my lip, and then yelped from the bite.

"Miss Critt? You okay?" Charlie glanced up at me, a flicker of concern in his eyes.

"Uh... yeah," I stammered, my gaze darting between him and Lydia's insistent specter. "It's just that—"

Lydia interrupted me again with a desperate plea. "He doesn't see me! Why can't he see me?"

My attention split between them like a rope fraying under

tension; I struggled to maintain any semblance of poise. "I know..."

"Know what? What do you know?" Charlie prompted again, his brow furrowing as he caught my erratic behavior.

"I know that...I mean, I wonder who...I..." I stammered, unable to formulate a question for Lydia that wouldn't make Charlie suspicious or think me crazier than he likely already did.

Taking a deep breath, I faced an impossible choice: continue this awkward charade or confess my secret ability to a potential non-believer.

"Charlie," I began hesitantly. "You should know something about me—something that makes this investigation... personal."

He closed Lydia's journal and looked up at me with those penetrating amber eyes that seemed to see right through my facade.

"I can see and speak to ghosts," I blurted out. The words hung like a misty exhale on a frosty morning.

Charlie blinked slowly; the gears behind those assessing eyes turned cautiously. "Ghosts?"

I nodded, swallowing hard against the lump forming in my throat. "Yes, and Lydia—she's here right now."

The room fell silent except for the distant chatter from Main Street filtering through the windows. Charlie stood motionless for what felt like an eternity before finally speaking.

"Behind me?"

I nodded again. "Yes."

He turned slowly, scanning the room with a skeptic's scrutiny before facing me again.

"I don't see anything," he mumbled.

Lydia grew more agitated now, gesturing wildly as if trying to break through an invisible barrier to make herself known.

"Tell him everything!" she implored.

"I know this is hard to believe," I told Charlie. "But ever since my fortieth birthday... I've been able to communicate with spirits. And Lydia,"—I gestured toward her ghost—" she needs help. And peace."

Charlie remained quiet for a moment before replying with careful deliberation. "Carrigan, I've heard from the other deputies that you do some incredible things."

A sliver of hope sparked within me at his words.

"But seeing ghosts... That's quite the claim." His skepticism was palpable, yet not entirely dismissive—a reaction better than outright disbelief.

"Look," I said earnestly. "I get how crazy it sounds. But if you trust me on anything—it's this."

Lydia's ghost pleaded once more for my attention. I directly addressed her spectral form with a sigh. "Lydia, what do you want to tell us?"

Charlie watched me in silent fascination as Lydia poured out a fragmented recollection that only I could hear and piece together.

"She says someone was arguing with her about something valuable.—something they wanted from her." My voice became more confident as Lydia spoke.

Charlie gave a small scoff. "Miss Critt, this is ridiculous. Are you trying to tell me you're speaking to Lydia Grant's ghost right now?"

I nodded. "Yes. Look, I don't expect you to believe me... please try."

Charlie let out a frustrated sigh. "Fine, I'll play along," he flipped through one journal. "She mentioned VV, MW, and a JR in the journals—does she remember anything about someone with those initials?" Charlie asked. His question didn't guarantee acceptance, but it buoyed me.

I asked Lydia the question directly while facing Charlie so he could follow along as best as he could.

She shook her head sadly.

"She can't conjure the memory, but I think the MW is for Marcia Wells," I began, recalling what she had said the night before. "And JR may be Julian Ravenscroft—Marcia's lawyer."

Charlie nodded and scribbled notes on his pad.

Lydia swept over to hover directly in front of me. "The secrets, Carrigan. I remember where I hid them!"

Eyebrows raised, I nodded, encouraging her to continue without alerting Charlie. If there were buried secrets, I'd want a first stab at them since Charlie wouldn't allow me to participate in the investigation.

"Behind the board, in the wall..." Lydia flitted over to point an ethereal finger at a place in the wood paneling.

I nodded again. Charlie caught the nod.

"Your *ghost* telling you anything I need to know?" his smirk infuriated me.

"Nothing at all." I pressed my lips into a firm line.

"Help me, please, Carrigan..." Lydia pleaded before fading away like mist under sunlight—the ephemeral connection severed without warning or satisfaction.

"Dammit!" My exasperation escaped before I could catch it. I opted for a quick recovery. "She's gone."

After another pause, Charlie regarded me with an unreadable expression. "This is unfamiliar territory for me," he admitted. "But let's say... hypothetically... that you're telling the truth about this gift of yours."

His use of 'hypothetically' stung, but perhaps it was progress after all.

Before I could continue and assure him my gift was genuine, a clatter at the front of the shop startled us both.

Charlie and I looked at each other.

"Who the heckin' heck could be here?" I asked. Charlie shrugged and silently edged closer to the doorway leading to

Lydia's shop. I followed. The wooden floorboards beneath my feet creaked in protest.

My eyes caught something—a shadow. Before I could even process whether it was a person or another ghost, Alfie growled, startling the shadowy figure who bolted towards the door with all the grace of a spooked cat at a dog show.

Charlie reacted swiftly and decisively. He lunged after the intruder with an athleticism that belied my capabilities. The door slammed shut behind the man as he made his escape.

"Charlie!" I called out after him as he yanked open the door and disappeared down the street in pursuit.

Shouts and the sounds of scurrying feet punctuated the day as Charlie chased after our unexpected guest. I squinted through the window but caught only glimpses of flailing limbs and the back of a coat before they vanished around a corner.

Minutes later, Charlie returned, panting from exertion, his face etched with frustration. "Slippery fellow," he said between breaths. "I couldn't catch him."

"Did you see who it was?" My voice was hopeful, though I knew identifying someone in such haste was a long shot at best.

He shook his head. "Not clearly. Did you?"

I shook my head. "No, not really, just an outline of his features. He ducked away rather quickly."

My mind raced as I tried to identify who it could've been. Someone Lydia had written about, perhaps? VV? JR? Each had potential reasons for being here, but fleeing like that added another mystery to a perplexing case.

Charlie began collecting Lydia's scattered journals from where we'd left them and bundled them with care. "I'll take these back to the station," Charlie said as he tucked them securely under his arm. "I'm going to drive around in my cruiser and see if I can spot our runner."

I nodded. "You go ahead. I'll lock up here."

"Here." Charlie handed me the key to the shop. "Thanks. Return it to the station when you can."

I opened my mouth to tell him I already had a key to the back door but thought better of it and shut my mouth. I watched him step out onto Main Street, where the daylight lit the sky innocently in contrast to our darkening situation.

—————

When Charlie's footsteps faded, I closed the door behind him and softly clicked the lock. As I shuffled into the back room, my fingers trembled with nerves and anticipation. Alfie padded ahead, his tail flicking. "All right, Lydia," I whispered, "let's see what you've hidden away."

The back room of the shop was a chaotic contrast to the organized front. Jars and bottles filled with creams, serums, and tinctures were scattered about the room, on shelves, and amid the paperwork on the desk. The earthy scent of essential oils lingered in the air.

"Lydia, are you still here?" I asked, as my gaze swept over every surface, seeking the anomaly Lydia's ghost had pointed toward.

And there it was—a patch on the wallboard that didn't quite match the rest, its edges slightly worn and askew. Heart pounding, I reached out and gave it a gentle push. It swung inward with a creak of protest, revealing a hidden nook within the wall.

I let out a breath I hadn't realized I'd been holding as I peered inside. Nestled within was a small, worn notebook—the kind that had seen years of use—and a stack of notecards bound by a frayed rubber band.

With hands as steady as an overly caffeinated jitterbug, I pulled out the notebook first. The pages were filled with meticulous handwriting detailing what appeared to be

Lydia's botanical formulas. There were notes in the margins, adjustments, and observations that spoke of countless hours of trial and error. Each entry was more than just a recipe; it was a piece of Lydia's soul poured onto paper.

My fingers then teased apart the notecards. But as I flipped through them, my brow furrowed in confusion. These weren't like the entries in the notebook; they listed ingredients that were anything but botanical—chemical names that twisted my tongue and sounded harsh to my ears.

"This doesn't make any sense," I muttered to myself. Lydia advocated for all things natural; she wouldn't dabble in synthetics. The cards felt foreign in my hands—out of place amidst her legacy.

I looked at Lydia's notebook and placed a note card beside it. There were distinguished differences in the writing. Lydia's writing was softer, with more loops, while the card lettering was definite, with solid lines and angular letters.

A realization hit me like a cold splash of water: these weren't Lydia's formulas; they belonged to someone else. But who? And why hide them here?

I scanned them again, searching for clues or initials that might reveal their owner. Nothing stood out—no scribbled notes or telltale signs—just cold, impersonal instructions for creating something far removed from Lydia's ethos.

"Looks like we've got another piece of this puzzle," I said aloud, though Alfie seemed more interested in an errant moth fluttering near one of the light fixtures. I carefully stuffed the notebook and notecards into my bag, ensuring they were secure.

With one last glance around the room to ensure we had missed nothing else, Alfie hopped back into his backpack carrier with an insistent "meow." He enjoyed being carted around like groceries but wasn't patient about the process.

"Okay, Mister Man," I reassured him as I zipped him in,

slung the backpack over my shoulder, and felt his weight settle against my back. "Let's head back to the festival. We've got a new puzzle to solve."

CHAPTER 9

MISSED & DISSED

THE FESTIVAL WAS a siren song of normalcy. People laughed and shared stories over cups of cider, not knowing the turmoil lurking around their comfortable little corner.

Every face seemed suspect as I walked through crowds of festival-goers to the management booth. Trixie sidled up beside me, her arms laden with bags of goodies from the various stalls. She dumped them on the table with a flourish, powdered sugar from a box of donuts puffing like a ghostly exhale.

"Looks like you've raided half the festival," I teased, eyeing the assortment of treats.

Trixie's eyes sparkled with mischief. "Can you blame me? The Ghostly Gallows' lemon tarts are to die for. Although, not as good as Lydia's..." Her voice trailed off, a shadow passing over her eyes, now glistening with tears.

I reached out, gently squeezing her shoulder. "Hey, it's okay. We'll figure this out. Lydia's ghost appeared while Charlie and I dug around her shop. I had to admit to him I could see ghosts. And Alfie found another clue," I said, stuffing a powdered sugar donut into my mouth. I peered around to ensure Mother wasn't about to ascend on me and scold me for my food choices.

"What did Alfie find this time?" Radleigh joined us, grabbing a piece of taffy and popping it into his mouth.

"Alfie found her teacup." I chugged a bottle of iced tea to wash the donut down. "It's likely how the arsenic was delivered. Charlie took the teacup into evidence for testing." My gaze shifted to the spot where Lydia's stall had stood. The tarp flapped mournfully in the breeze, and empty tables haunted the space beneath.

Trixie sat down and leaned forward, elbows on the table, chin resting on her fists. "What did Charlie say when you told him you could see ghosts?"

"I don't think he believed me." I closed my eyes momentarily, recalling the spectral image of Lydia and the conversation with Charlie. "Lydia's ghost was still confused, so I couldn't give him much information, which probably made it worse. But she pointed at a secret hiding spot in the wall just before a mysterious man burst in, and Charlie gave chase." I opened my eyes to find Trixie's concerned gaze locked on mine.

"Really?" she asked. "Who was it?"

"I'm not sure. Charlie tried to catch him, but he got away. He's driving around now, trying to find him."

"Curious." Trixie pursed her lips thoughtfully. "Marcia has to know something." She popped a piece of fudge into her mouth. "We know she's involved from her initials in the journals, and Lydia's ghost confirmed it," she said—her mouth full of chocolaty goodness. "Maybe this mystery man has something to do with Lydia's death. Ooh! Maybe he's a hired killer!"

"Or, he could have been someone who knew she died and was just there to steal stuff," Radleigh piped up.

My hand brushed against the smooth surface of the notecards tucked safely inside my jacket. "After Charlie gave chase, I found these in Lydia's hiding spot. I'm willing to bet this is what all the hullabaloo is about." With a careful motion, I pulled out the stack and laid it on the table.

Trixie and Radleigh leaned in, their expressions a mix of curiosity and concern. Trixie's fingers danced hesitantly above the cards before she plucked one from the top. Her eyes scanned the angular script detailing an intricate blend of toxins.

"Boron, Formaldehyde, and Polyethylene Glycol." she read aloud, her voice trailing into silence as she absorbed the significance of each ingredient. "And Mercury?"

"These are her secret formulas?" Radleigh breathed, his gaze flitting across the words like a hummingbird darting between blooms.

"No. The formulas on the cards are not Lydia's. Here." I pulled out Lydia's notebook and showed it to my team. "See? Natural ingredients. I'm assuming her entire formulation is in this notebook."

"The ones Marcia would kill to get her hands on for her new botanical line," Radleigh murmured.

I shivered at his choice of words—' would kill.' "We can't jump to conclusions," I cautioned, even as my mind reeled with possibilities. "Even these," I spread out the note cards that contained the toxic and synthetic ingredients, "could be motives for anyone wanting to edge Lydia out of business."

"Or someone who thought Lydia had something that didn't belong to her," Trixie suggested, her brow furrowed as she searched the cards before putting them back on the pile.

I nodded. "Exactly. The question is: who wrote these formulas, and why did Lydia have them?"

"And who knew that Lydia had them? And was the mysterious man after them?" Radleigh tapped his finger against his lips, pondering.

"It's possible the mysterious man was just a hired thief by any of her competition," Trixie mused. "Even employees, friends... or family."

"Family?" Rad echoed with a quizzical tilt of his head.

"Robert Grant," I said softly, rolling his name around like one might taste a bitter flavor. "Lydia's husband. But why would he need to hire someone to steal these?"

"Maybe to sell them to the highest bidder?" Rad offered.

"Ooh! Sell them to Marcia!" Trixie vibrated with a sugar rush.

We all fell silent as we contemplated this new angle. Then Alfie jumped onto my lap, purring as if he knew we were onto something important and wanted in on the action.

"Wait. What about Liz?" Trixie's voice cut through our thoughts like a scalpel.

"Liz?" I repeated. The gears in my head started turning faster now. "But why would Liz... unless she's not just Marcia's assistant?"

"You think there's more to her than meets the cat-eye?" Radleigh asked, fluttering his lashes.

"It wouldn't be the first time someone played double agent in a murder," I mused.

"And there were initials in Lydia's journals that we didn't recognize," Trixie pointed out, her fingers tapping rhythmically on the table—a telltale sign she was piecing things together just as rapidly.

I leaned forward, lowering my voice despite our seclusion beneath the tent. "VV... Liz's last name is Vincent." A chill shimmied through me. "But her initials are EV—E for Elizabeth...but maybe..."

Radleigh gasped softly while Trixie sat up straighter. "You think Liz could be behind this? But that means—"

"—she might be working with someone else or for her gain," I finished for her. My head swam with questions, motives swirling around like leaves caught in a fall gust. "But who?"

"Let's not get ahead of ourselves," Radleigh cautioned gently. He was right; conjecture wouldn't solve this case—facts would.

I exhaled slowly and collected myself before continuing. "For now, let's focus on what we know." I fanned out the formula cards like tarot cards foretelling our next move.

"The lipstick tube found near Lydia... could that have been planted to frame Marcia?" Trixie wondered aloud as she glanced at me for affirmation or rebuttal.

"It's possible," I conceded. My mind returned to Charlie's news about the small traces of arsenic in the lipstick. "Charlie confirmed there wasn't enough poison in the lipstick to kill. Perhaps the killer didn't realize that when he or she planted the tube?"

"If it was planted, then someone was trying to cover his or her tracks," Rad concluded with grim certainty.

Trixie bit her lip. "We need to find out more about Liz..."

"We do," I agreed. Alfie stretched across my lap then, as if trying to soothe the tension knotting within me.

"But how? We can't exactly waltz over to Marcia's table and demand answers—not without more evidence." Radleigh mumbled, chewing on another piece of taffy.

"We'll start by determining what these formulas mean for Lydia's business and whether Marcia stands to benefit from their theft or replication." My voice held an edge of weariness.

"I'll talk to Eunice and see what I can dig up around town." Trixie offered.

"And I'll charm whatever information I can out of our festival attendees—discreetly," Radleigh said. "Maybe others have overheard something they didn't realize was important."

An older woman approached our table with hesitant steps and an aura of lavender and mothballs. Radleigh greeted her with his usual charm, but I could tell by how he held a finger under his nose that he smelled the nasty array of her perfume.

My gaze moved from the woman clutching her handbag like a lifeline to a commotion at Marcia's table.

Stepping outside the management tent, I witnessed a rather handsome, tall gentleman with his arm wrapped around Marcia. Their display seemed rather…intimate.

Standing before them was Robert Grant, his face red with anger. He was shouting something at Marcia and the man she was with, and it appeared Marcia was trying to calm Robert down.

Then, the handsome man pulled his arm away from Marcia and went rather red-faced as well. Both men raised their voices at Marcia and each other.

My eyes wavered over the three until something off to one side snagged my attention. Another tall man, wearing dark jeans and a black hoodie, observed the trio some feet away.

My heart skipped at the sight of him.

"That's the man that was rummaging Lydia's shop!" I fumbled with my phone to call Charlie. This could be the break we needed. But before I could continue, an ear-splitting crash erupted from behind us.

We spun around to find one of our banners had toppled over, taking a part of our display with it. Radleigh sprang into action, deftly righting the banner and offering apologies with humor to calm any startled onlookers.

When I looked back, the man was gone, as were Robert and the handsome man, leaving an exasperated-looking Marcia alone at her table.

"Hello? Hello?" I heard Charlie's voice on the phone.

"Charlie! That man was just here, at the festival!"

"Keep an eye out. I'm on my way."

"He's gone." I cried.

"I'll be right there." Charlie hung up.

I exchanged glances with Trixie and Radleigh; we didn't need words to express our collective frustration—or determination.

"We should try to find him," Trixie declared.

"We'll split up," Radleigh suggested after a moment's thought. His face was set in determined lines, usually reserved for his fiercest drag performances as 'Luna Eclipse.'

I gave them both an appreciative nod; "Meet back here in a few minutes," I instructed as we prepared to disperse into the sea of festivities.

As I rushed through the crowd, my mind raced with possibilities—each more unnerving than the last.

A few minutes stretched into what seemed like hours as we trudged back to Marcia's table, spirits low and bodies weary. We had scoured every nook and cranny of the bustling grounds, yet the elusive mystery man had yet to turn up. The echo of laughter and music swirled around us, a contrast to the knotted anxiety in my stomach.

"Nothing, huh?" Charlie appeared, his voice sliced through the clamor as he approached, brows furrowed in concern.

I shook my head, trying to mask my frustration with a half-hearted smile. "He vanished like a ghost; trust me, I'd know."

Charlie's gaze lingered on me a moment longer than necessary. My chest heaved from the recent excursion as much as it did from Charlie's gaze. He reached a hand out toward my face, and I instinctively pushed my cheek into his warm palm, as Alfie does to me. I held my breath.

This was it.

We were having a 'moment'.

"Uh, Carrigan, you have a little something…"

"Yes, I feel it too," I said, mistaking his meaning.

"…Powder of some kind." His finger touched the side of my mouth…

"Oh! I...yes, from the donut. Oh, goodness." My cheeks flushed as I brushed away the offensive telltale from my face.

"Got it. You and donuts don't quite agree, it seems." Charlie chuckled, reminding me of the Heimlich incident from the day before.

My cheeks burned. Thankfully, Trixie and Radleigh interrupted us.

Radleigh caught the shift in my demeanor, a knowing glint in his eye betraying his amusement. "Easy there, Carrie. You're fluttering like a flag at a pride parade."

I shot him a glare that lacked any actual heat. "Hush, you."

Charlie tipped an imaginary hat toward Radleigh and Trixie and gave me a little wink that sent my heart into A-Fib. I momentarily hoped the first-aid station had a set of chest paddles. I'd likely need them to restart my heart.

Before I could make introductions, Radleigh interjected. "And who might this vision of law enforcement be?"

I gestured between them. "Charlie Best, meet Radleigh Moon and Trixie Hawthorne. Radleigh assists me at the funeral home, and Trixie owns the craft shop in town."

Radleigh pushed past Trixie and offered his hand with a flourish, his rings catching the light like tiny disco balls, his flirtatious nature on full display. "A pleasure to meet you, Deputy Best."

Charlie's handshake was firm but not overpowering—an equal match to Radleigh's enthusiasm.

"The pleasure is mine," he said, shaking Trixie's hand. "Thank you for your help in this matter. Where did you first see the man, Miss Critt?"

"He was watching a rather heated exchange at Marcia Well's booth."

"A heated exchange?"

"Yes, between Marcia, Robert Grant, and a rather handsome fellow that seemed to have Marcia's attention—if you get my meaning."

Charlie quirked a brow and nodded slowly. "Great, thanks. I'll go ask Marcia a few questions."

"I'm coming with you." Before Charlie could protest, I pushed past him and headed toward Marcia's table, Radleigh, Trixie, and Alfie following close behind.

CHAPTER 10
PREP & PRANCE

WE NAVIGATED through clusters of festival-goers, each step heightening the tension that clung to our little group like the evening mist rolling in from the sea. Marcia stood behind her table. The handsome fellow and Robert Grant were nowhere in sight.

"Marcia!" I called out, fast approaching. Marcia, who had been talking with Liz, whipped her head around in my direction.

Charlie sidled up beside me. I made a quick introduction, and Charlie didn't waste a second. "Miss Wells, a man was seen close to your table earlier. He was tall and wearing dark clothing. Did you see him?"

Marcia flicked an imaginary speck of dust from her Trend Savvy display before meeting Charlie's gaze with practiced ease. "I'm afraid I don't know whom you're referring to."

I arched an eyebrow, skeptical. "Are you sure? He was standing just there," I motioned to the spot where I had seen him, "he was watching you argue with Robert and the handsome fellow with his arm around your waist, whose name is…?" I tried to push for an answer.

Marcia flushed. "Whose name is none of your business." She straightened.

Charlie flipped his notebook open. "Miss Wells, where were you the night Lydia Grant died?"

Her eyes locked onto Charlie's with unwavering confidence. "I had to leave town for a meeting."

"Where was the meeting?"

Marcia paused, her eyes flicking from Charlie to me, then her table. She straightened up. "At my office in Portland."

My heart thumped erratically against my ribs—a rhythm of realization and disbelief. I turned to Charlie. "That's where Robert Grant told me he was."

Charlie flipped through the pages of his notepad with deliberate slowness, his eyes scanning his notes before lifting to meet mine.

"Yes, right," he confirmed quietly, the word hanging heavy in the cooling air. "Miss Wells, I'm taking you to the station for questioning."

Radleigh, Trixie, and I watched Charlie lead a semi-cooperative Marcia from the Festival grounds. We turned back to the table, where Liz was busy moving products and restocking the table.

"Liz…Elizabeth…Vincent…" I started with what I hoped was a comforting purr. Trixie and Radleigh leaned against the table, knowing exactly what I was about to ask and eager to hear the answers.

Liz glanced at me sideways before turning to face me. "Carrigan. Lovely to see you." Her smile seemed forced, but I ignored it.

"Liz, do you know who had his arm wrapped around Marcia earlier?"

Liz paused. Her lips curved into a sly smile. "That must have been Julian Ravenscroft, Marcia's solicitor."

I could sense Radleigh and Trixie vibrating beside me.

"They appeared to be quite…intimate. Is it safe to assume their relationship is…more than professional?"

Liz raised an eyebrow. "That's not any of my business—or yours," she lowered her voice to a conspiratorial whisper, "but yes, they are *involved.*"

I nodded. "And do you know what the argument with Robert Grant was about?"

"I'm afraid I wasn't here to witness any argument. I was back at my car, getting more supplies." She waved a hand toward the freshly opened boxes of products.

"Ah, yes. The Trend Savvy products." I picked up a face wash tube and squinted, reading the fine print of the ingredients. Radleigh and Trixie did the same.

The products contained many of the toxic ingredients listed on the notecards. But most synthetic cosmetics use the same ingredients, so it didn't mean that the notecards belonged to Marcia. "Liz, you're Marcia's chemist, right?"

Liz peered at me. "Yes, why?"

"Are these ingredients common in most cosmetics?" I turned a tube of face cream toward her.

She squinted. "There are similarities and differences between every brand and every company. We use them to perform certain functions in the formula, such as binding ingredients together."

I nodded. "I see. And you keep detailed notes on the formulas?"

Liz looked at me like I was the dumbest person on the planet. "Of *course*, I keep detailed notes."

"On notecards? Or…"

"What? Why are you asking?"

"Oh, just curious," I replied, plastering my best, brightest smile. "I'm fascinated by the process, is all. So you keep note cards? And do you keep them locked up like state secrets?"

Liz eyed me. "I don't keep notecards, no. But my formulas are kept in a very safe place."

"Ah, I see. Well, that's very good, then. Trixie? Radleigh? We should get back to our duties. It's a pleasure to speak to you today, Liz." I pivoted, then stopped abruptly when I saw the Queen of Cicadas herself headed straight toward me.

My mother.

Standing before Marcia's booth, I felt the scrutiny before seeing her—the weight of a gaze that could slice through steel. Mother's impeccable posture, a column of pure matriarchal might, drew an unmistakable line in the air as she approached. She gave Radleigh and Trixie air kisses before looking me up and down.

"Carrie, my dear, you must get home and prepare for the gala." Her eyes roved over my ensemble as if it were a crime scene. "And find something decent to wear!"

I glanced down at my clothes, the familiar comfort of my faded jeans and cozy sweater suddenly feeling like an embarrassment. "The gala? Mother, what are you talking about? I wasn't planning on—"

"Nonsense!" she waved her hand, her bracelets clinking like a symphony of disapproval. "You're going, and that's final. We'll find you a gown to highlight your best…features." She said as she attempted to pull and tuck my shirt into my jeans.

"Mother, stop it!" I stepped back from Marcia's booth, distancing myself from Liz's prying ears. "Mother, I don't think it's necessary—"

But Mother was a force unto herself, not easily swayed by protests or logic. "You will go to the Gala," she insisted, her voice leaving no room for argument. "And meet that handsome lawyer, Julian Ravenscroft!"

The name sent a ripple through me. According to Liz, Julian was Marcia's sharp-dressed confidant and partner in whatever skullduggery they were cooking up.

Maybe going to the gala wasn't such a bad idea.

I hesitated only for a moment before acquiescing with a

sigh. If getting dolled up was what it took to hobnob with Julian and pry some answers loose, then so be it. "Fine," I conceded, much to Mother's delight.

Mother turned on her heel with a victorious smile and left to hunt down a gown suitable for her daughter—a task she relished more than any art collection or social event.

As she swanned off on her mission, Radleigh's laugh rang out like a church bell in celebration. Trixie joined in. Her laugh was softer but no less amused.

"Oh, honey," Radleigh managed between chuckles, his Texas drawl thick with mirth. "You strutting into that gala in full glam? I'd pay good money to see that!"

I rolled my eyes but couldn't suppress the grin tugging at my lips. "Laugh it up, Moon Pie," I said, giving him a playful shove. "But if I'm going to interrogate Julian Ravenscroft, I must blend in with the snobbery."

Trixie beamed at me. "Carrigan, it's a fabulous idea. You'll be like a ghost whisperer turned Bond girl!"

I snorted at the thought. Me? A Bond girl? It's more like Bond's klutzy cousin twice removed. But if it got me closer to unraveling this rigmarole of murder and mystery, I'd channel my inner spy with all the enthusiasm I could muster.

We wandered away from Marcia's booth, checked on our volunteers at the management booth, and headed toward my little brick cottage.

"Alright," I began as we walked, Alfie trotting loyally at my side. "If I'm going undercover at this shindig, we need a game plan."

Radleigh hummed thoughtfully, twirling a lock of his vibrantly dyed wig around his finger. "First things first, darling," he said with the authority of a general leading troops into battle. "We need to get you looking the part."

"Rad's right," Trixie agreed with a nod. "You need to look so stunning that Julian won't suspect you're there for anything other than the champagne and chitchat."

A tingle of excitement raced up my spine at the prospect of dressing up and playing detective amidst Castle Point's elite. But there was also that niggling feeling in the pit of my stomach—the fear that I'd stick out like a sore thumb or, worse, trip over my own two feet and take down an entire buffet table.

"We've got your back," Trixie said as if reading my mind.

"I'll do your makeup," Radleigh chimed in with gusto. "And not just any makeup—we're talking high-definition perfection that'll make you glow like the goddess you are."

"And I'll help with your hair," Trixie offered eagerly. "Something elegant but simple."

Their enthusiasm was infectious; it swelled within me until it felt like I could actually pull this off.

Radleigh rushed to the funeral home to retrieve his makeup case while Trixie and I waited outside. When we reached my house, plans were in full swing. We piled into my cozy living room and got down to business.

"So," Radleigh began as he pulled out an array of eyeshadow palettes that looked more complex than my fancy espresso maker, which I still can't get the hang of. "We'll keep your look classic—think Grace Kelly meets Morticia Addams."

I chuckled at the thought of those two style icons somehow merging into one person—me.

"And don't worry about dancing or anything like that," Trixie added while sorting through her extensive collection of hairpins and clips. "You just focus on Julian and getting information out of him."

I nodded, though part of me—a tiny part—wondered what it would be like to dance without stepping on someone's toes.

"Okay then," I said, "let's make sure this isn't all for naught."

Radleigh and Trixie worked their magic as we prepared

for the evening ahead. With each brush stroke from Radleigh and every twist and pin from Trixie's deft fingers, my usual guise melted away, replaced by someone who might just fit in among Castle Point's glitterati—or at least not spill canapés down her dress within the first five minutes.

Mother swept into my cottage like a hurricane of taffeta and pearls, a garment bag clutched in her well-manicured hands. "Carrigan, darling, prepare to be transformed," she announced with a flourish that would've made a Broadway star envious.

I stood halfway between excitement and dread. Sensing the heightened drama, Alfie darted under the sofa.

"Mother," I said, bracing myself for whatever confection of lace and ruffles she bought. "You know I'm not the gown type. Can't I wear a nice pair of black slacks and a blouse?"

"Nonsense," she scolded, her tone leaving no room for argument as she unzipped the garment bag with a dramatic hiss. "Every woman can be a goddess if properly attired."

The dress that emerged from the bag was stunning. It was a deep emerald green that would make the pine trees envious. Its simple yet elegant cut promised to accentuate rather than exaggerate.

I couldn't help the gasp that escaped me. "Mother, it's... it's beautiful."

Morgana beamed, clearly pleased with herself. "I knew it would be perfect for you. Although, it took the saleswoman ages to find one in your size." she drolled, "Now, let's get you into it."

With Trixie and Radleigh's help—after the first higgledy-piggledy wiggling into a full bodysuit of Spanx—I slipped into the gown. It hugged my curves in all the right places and fell to the floor in a gentle cascade of fabric.

Mother clasped her hands together as if witnessing a miracle. "Carrigan, you look—"

"—like I should sip martinis with James Bond?" I quipped,

unable to resist the joke even as I admired my reflection in the mirror.

"Well, let's not get carried away." She corrected with a smirk that mirrored my own. "Even Mr. Bond has his standards."

Radleigh circled me like an artist admiring his masterpiece. "A touch more blush," he mused aloud, dabbing at my cheeks softly.

Trixie stepped back to assess their handiwork. "A vision," she declared with a satisfied nod.

I felt different—stronger somehow as if the dress was armor and makeup my war paint. As Radleigh applied the finishing touches and Trixie adjusted every pin in my hair, I turned to face them and felt a rush of gratitude for this motley crew of allies.

"Thank you," I said sincerely. "For everything."

"There's nothing we wouldn't do for you," Trixie replied, warmth radiating from her smile.

Radleigh gave me one final once-over before nodding in approval. "Now go out there and shine like the star you are."

Mother stepped forward then, her demeanor softening as she took my hands. "Carrigan, make no mistake—you will turn Julian's head tonight. Your father would be so proud."

Mother's sincere compliment and rare mention of my late father momentarily stunned me. Bravely venting out from his hiding place, Alfie meowed his agreement, bringing me back to reality. I took a deep breath and prepared to enter the high society spotlight.

Dressed to impress with nerves jangling beneath my poised exterior, I faced my reflection—a beautiful stranger looking back at me with determination etched onto her features.

It was showtime.

CHAPTER 11
GALA & GOONS

THE GALA WAS HELD at The Pointe—a grand estate overlooking the ocean, with gardens so manicured they looked painted on. As we approached the entrance, fairy lights twinkled like stars coming down to play among us mortals.

The grand ballroom was abuzz with conversation and laughter as Castle Point's finest gathered in all their sartorial splendor. A quartet played classical music that floated above our heads like gossamer threads binding us together at this moment of celebration.

As Mother and I entered the room arm-in-arm, a waiter offered us glasses of champagne on a silver platter. Mother readily accepted hers, as she had been born into countless social gatherings such as this one. For some bizarre reason, I felt a bow of thanks was necessary—effectively spilling most of my glass's contents on the floor at the waiter's feet—warranting my mother's exasperated and overly dramatic eye roll.

"Carrigan," she whispered harshly, "keep your wits about you. We're at a Gala, not some back-alley honkytonk."

"I'm sorry, Mother. I'm just so nervous!" I replied under

my breath, my cheeks burning. Mother waved me off and joined her peers while I ventured deeper into the crowd.

My heart beat a staccato rhythm against my ribs—whether from nerves or excitement, I couldn't tell. I did my best to sashay around the room, reasonably sure I looked more like an elegant trash bag billowing in the wind than the graceful, delicate princess I aimed to be. Then I spotted Julian.

He stood near a fireplace mantel adorned with fresh flowers and antique candelabras, and his laughter reached me even before I drew near enough to join his circle. The handsome lawyer wore confidence like a second skin—and why wouldn't he? He had looks, brains, and now Marcia Wells' attention as she clung to his arm like ivy on an old stone wall.

As the circle dispersed, Julian's demeanor toward Marcia changed. He appeared desperate to shake her off, treating her like a pesky summer mosquito. His disdain was apparent, a stark contrast to the display of affection I had witnessed before the argument between Marcia, Julian, and Robert began. I wondered if Julian's irritation with Marcia then was causing him to withhold his affection now.

I steeled myself before approaching them; Marcia's sharp eyes found mine immediately and couldn't contain her shock.

"Carrigan Critt," Marcia greeted me coolly. I must say you look different tonight."

"That's sort of the point," I said smoothly while extending a hand for an obligatory greeting. Marcia ignored my hand and greeted Mother—who had silently joined our trio—with a warmth and affection she didn't share with me.

"Who are your lovely friends, Marcia?" Julian turned his charm toward Mother and me, who responded with equal poise and grace.

As pleasantries were exchanged over champagne flutes and delicate canapés, I watched Marcia closely for any sign that would betray her guilt or innocence regarding Lydia's death.

But Marcia Wells was adept at keeping her emotions under lock and key—a skill set I suspected extended far beyond business dealings into much darker realms.

The music shifted to a waltz, and Julian extended his hand to me with an elegance that suggested he was as confident on the dance floor as he was in the courtroom. "May I have this dance?" he asked.

I hesitated; the image of my two left feet stumbling like clumsy baby goats trying to jump over each other flashed before me. "I should warn you, I'm not exactly graceful," I confessed.

His smile broadened. "Nonsense. I'll lead."

Taking a deep breath, I placed my hand in his and let him guide me onto the dance floor. Julian's touch was firm, and despite my usual clumsiness, he steered me with such finesse that I twirled and stepped without incident.

As we danced, I tried to match the rhythm of our conversation to the tempo of the music. "So, Julian, you and Marcia seem quite close," I ventured, testing the waters.

"I suppose we are," he replied smoothly. "We've worked together for quite some time."

"Ah, yes. I understand you're her solicitor, helping manage her Trend Savvy Empire." Julian nodded as he expertly led me around the dance floor. "I saw you two at the festival earlier," I continued, "there seemed to be some... tension."

Julian's expression flickered ever so slightly, his eyes darkening as he glanced over at Marcia, who was now engaged in animated discussion with another guest. "Business partnerships have their difficulties," he said cryptically.

The waltz brought us closer to Marcia's orbit. Julian gazed at her with a mix of disdain and something more mysterious.

"Marcia's quite a force to be reckoned with," I said, pushing further while attempting a step that felt more like a stumble. Julian steadied me with a gentle but firm grip on my waist.

"Indeed she is," he replied, his voice low and controlled.

As we glided across the floor—me desperately trying not to trample on Julian's polished shoes—I pondered my next move. The gala was an opportunity too golden to waste; if Julian knew something about Lydia's death or Marcia's involvement, now was the time to coax it out of him.

"Marcia mentioned an important meeting in Portland the night Lydia Grant passed." I left the sentence hanging as we spun beneath the crystal chandelier.

Julian's eyes met mine again; this time, there was no mistaking the flash of confusion that passed through them before he composed himself. "Yes, business often calls us away at inconvenient times."

Did he not know of Marcia's trip to Portland? Our dance continued amidst laughter and clinking glasses around us, an elegant charade we were all too aware of playing. With each step and turn, I tried another angle—another question aimed at unraveling the mystery that had brought us all here tonight.

"So, you were with Marcia in Portland the night of Lydia's death?" I asked innocently enough.

Julian raised an eyebrow. "No, I was not," he hissed. He glanced over at Marcia, his eyes revealing confusion and irritation.

"Then, may I ask where you were the night of Lydia's death?"

A polite smile played on his lips as he executed a flawless spin without toppling me entirely. "I was here, in Castle Point, visiting my Mother."

I opened my mouth to press further when we were interrupted by Marcia, who cut in with a practiced smile. "May I steal him away? There are matters we need to discuss."

I stepped back reluctantly, relinquishing Julian's hand, but not without noting the briefest exchange between them: her tight-lipped urgency against his barely concealed annoyance.

As they departed toward a quieter corner of the room for their private tête-à-tête, I stood among the twirling couples, feeling both flummoxed and intrigued by Julian and Marcia's 'relationship'—and more determined than ever to find out what secrets lay beneath their glittering surface.

I extricated myself from the dance floor, the graceful whirl of the waltz giving way to a room still pulsing with the thrum of a hundred conversations. My gaze flitted across the crowd, a glittering tapestry of Castle Point's elite until it snagged on a familiar figure.

This mysterious man who had fled Lydia's shop was standing by the bar, clad in a tuxedo that seemed to bolster his commanding presence.

———

My heart skipped a staccato beat. I reached into my pocketbook for my phone to call Charlie, then thought better of it. If I could get close enough to the mysterious figure to talk to him, I would have a better chance of getting answers than if Charlie dragged him off to the station for questioning.

He stood alone, sipping champagne with the casual air of an observer rather than a participant, his eyes fixed on Marcia and Julian—now deep in conversation. Their exchange had taken on an edge. Their voices pitched just low enough to evade eavesdropping but with body language that spoke volumes—a rigid stance from Marcia, Julian's index finger chopping the air for emphasis.

Curiosity piqued, I navigated my way through clusters of chatting guests. With each step closer to my target, I could see his features more clearly—sharp angles softened by the amber glow of chandeliers. A bead of condensation rolled down his glass as he lifted it to his lips.

As I reached him, Julian and Marcia broke apart abruptly; she stalked off in one direction while he disappeared into another, leaving ripples of tension in their wake.

"Excuse me," I called out gently, not wanting to startle him as he moved to leave. "I'm Carrigan Critt."

His eyes narrowed briefly. "Victor Venn," he replied with a nod.

Victor Venn? VV! The initials from Lydia's journals! She must have been referring to the man standing before me. Otherwise, what business would he have snooping around Lydia's shop?

I extended my hand, and he took it in a firm grip. "You're not from around here," I observed, trying to contain my excitement at finding this new connection.

"That's correct," Victor said, releasing my hand as if he couldn't wait to remove the contact. "I'm from Portland."

Portland—just like Marcia and Julian—and initially, Lydia. The connection sent a ripple through me. "And what do you do in Portland?"

Victor's eyes looked at me, assessing. "I'm a genealogist."

"A genealogist? How interesting. So what brings you to our little gala?" I inquired with as much casualness as I could muster.

"Business," he replied tersely.

I tilted my head slightly, studying him. "Would that business have anything to do with Marcia Wells or Julian Ravenscroft?" And what kind of 'business' could a genealogist *have* with Marcia and Julian? I wanted to ask.

His gaze flickered toward the door through which Marcia had vanished moments ago, his jaw tightening at mentioning their names. He took another sip of champagne before answering. "Possibly."

The cryptic response hung between us like smoke; it wasn't an admission, but it wasn't denial either.

"And would this business be related to what you were

searching for at Lydia Grant's shop?" I pressed on, trying a tactic of surprise.

Recognition flashed in Victor's eyes—met squarely with mine now. He seemed to weigh his options before speaking again. "Miss Critt," he began carefully, "there are things at play here—histories and grievances that stretch further back than you might realize."

Histories and grievances—I knew those words all too well in this town where past and present were often indistinguishable. "I know Castle Point has its share of skeletons," I said more confidently than I felt. "But right now, I'm more interested in the flesh-and-blood variety—the kind that walks and talks... and sometimes kills."

Victor regarded me with an intensity that made me wonder just how much he knew about those skeletons—literal or otherwise.

"Mr. Venn, where were you the night Lydia Grant was murdered?"

"I had nothing to do with Lydia's demise, Miss Critt. I don't deal with death," he stated flatly.

"No?" My voice rose slightly in disbelief. "Then what do you deal with?"

Victor glanced around the room as if searching for unseen ears among the revelers before leaning closer. His breath carried a hint of the champagne he'd been nursing as he whispered conspiratorially, "Family secrets."

Secrets—an apparent currency more valuable than gold in this case.

"Is that why you were rummaging through Lydia's shop? To find her secrets?" I asked.

Victor straightened up and gave me a long look that seemed to size me up—a sleuth versus whatever role he played in this twisted narrative we'd all become part of.

"Well, if I told you, it wouldn't be a secret, would it? Let's say they involve old formulas and even older betrayals," he said cryptically before adding with sudden directness, "and if you're smart—which I believe you are—you'll stay out of it."

But staying out of it was never an option for me—not when there was a ghost waiting for justice and a killer still at large.

"Old formulas?" I echoed, thinking back to the chemical formulas scribbled on note cards tucked safely away from prying eyes.

Victor gave nothing away but raised his glass in a silent toast before taking one last gulp of his drink.

"Well," I said after a moment's pause filled only by the lilting strains of music that seemed so at odds with our conversation, "if you ever feel like sharing those secrets—"

"I'm sure I could find you," Victor finished for me with an enigmatic smile. "You seem the type that wouldn't be hard to miss," he finished, looking me up and down before excusing himself and melting into the crowd.

Left alone amidst swirling gowns and dapper suits, I felt both exhilarated and uneasy. Victor Venn had offered tantalizing hints wrapped in veiled warnings, threads waiting to be pulled in an ever-growing tapestry of mystery surrounding Lydia Grant's death.

And pull them I would—for Lydia's sake and my curiosity that wouldn't let me rest until every secret was dragged into the light.

CHAPTER 12
STITCH & STRAIGHTEN

WHEN I ARRIVED HOME, dancing my way up the path to the front door, I stopped short. The door was open a crack, and there were no lights on inside.

"Radleigh? Trix? You guys still here?" I pushed the door open slightly and reached a hand inside. Finding the light switch, I flicked it on and gasped.

Pushing the door open, I saw my home in shambles. The sofa had turned over, and the cushions had been chucked every which way. Books had been thrown off the bookcase and laid open on the floor. The entire living room had been upended.

"Radleigh? Trixie? Oh my God, Alfie? Alfie!" I cried out, stepping over the mess in search of life forms.

A solid meow came from the kitchen. I raced to the source and found Alfie sitting by his bowl, seemingly unfazed by anything but the growling of his stomach.

At the sight of me, Alfie began his insistent mewing, scooting under my gown and wrapping himself around my legs. "I know. I'm sorry I'm late. No excuses. But Alfie, what happened? Who was here?" I asked, leaning down to grab him. He momentarily panicked as he attempted to remove himself from the confines of my gown. Poking his head out from under, he peered up at me, meowed at the indecency of it all. I scooped him up and inspected him for signs of mistreatment. Thankfully, there wasn't any.

Once he was fed, I stepped carefully through the house, inspecting every room. Each one was in disarray. The drawers in my bedroom had also been torn from the chest, clothes strewn about. My office took the brunt of the storm. Drawers were open, papers littered the floor, and even the trash can was emptied; its contents pecked through.

Sighing, I texted the group chat with Trix and Rad, knowing they would have left their phones on, excited for gala updates.

"Guys, please get over here asap. Someone's been in my house!"

"What? OMG. OMW." Trixie replied.

"OMG OMG OMG. B there ASAP." Rad messaged.

Then, I called Charlie.

A deep, sleepy, dreamy, gruff voice answered. "Best."

"Charlie. It's Carrigan Critt. Someone ransacked my house!"

"What? Okay. Don't touch anything. Be right there."

I gave him my address and hung up.

The only thing still standing was my favorite armchair, so I nestled into its welcome embrace while waiting for my friends to arrive. Just as I sat, Trixie and Radleigh rushed in, gasping.

"Oh my word, Carrie! Are you okay?" Radleigh rushed to my side, tripping over books on the way.

"I'm fine. Just a bit shocked."

Alfie joined us from the kitchen, jumping on the tipped-over sofa. Trixie stroked his fur. "Oh, thank goodness Alfie's okay."

"Yes, thank goodness."

"Carrie, what do you think they were looking for?" Rad asked.

I reached into my bag. "Pretty sure, these." I pulled out the notecards. "I had them in my bag this whole time, in the hearse."

Charlie walked into the front door, and a deputy trailed behind him. I hastily shoved the cards back into my bag.

"Miss Critt, are you okay?" Charlie so kindly asked as he glanced at the dishevelment with a look of concern on his features. At Charlie's command, the deputy went to work dusting the doorknob and chosen articles strewn about the house for fingerprints.

"I'm a bit…shocked."

"Any idea why someone would do this? What they were looking for?" he asked.

I glanced at my bag and was about to reach for the note-cards when I thought better of it. Knowing Charlie didn't want me involved with the investigation and would have to take them into evidence, I would no longer have the opportunity to use them to uncover the mysteries they held.

"No idea, unfortunately. But I can assure you, my lady garments are safe."

Charlie raised an eyebrow. "Good to know. Any thoughts about who could have done this?" He took out his notepad and flipped it open to a new page.

"I do, actually. The individuals mentioned in Lydia's journals would be my first choice. Marcia Wells and Julian Ravenscroft, in particular. Also, I think I have figured out whose initials are 'VV.'"

"Oh?"

"Yes, Victor Venn. Who I also believe to be the mysterious man who was rummaging through Lydia's shop."

"The same man you saw at the festival grounds later?" Charlie asked.

"Yes, the same. I saw him at the gala this evening. That's

right, I was at a gala. I do 'fancy people' things, in case you were wondering why I look so magnificent this evening. This isn't my usual evening attire. However, I think perhaps it should be. Have you seen how my rear end looks in this thing?" I stood up and turned my rump towards Charlie, like a baboon presenting itself to its mate.

"Um… Yes, Miss Critt. But you were saying…about Victor Venn?"

"Oh, yes, that's right. I met him at the fancy-pants gala this evening and introduced myself."

"You what?" Radleigh and Trixie asked in unison.

"I said: I met…"

Radleigh waved a hand at my face. "We heard what you said, Carrigan."

Charlie agreed. "Yes, we heard. But my question is, why didn't you call me rather than introduce yourself to a potentially dangerous man?"

'Well, you see, deputy, I bask in the glory of danger whenever possible."

"Carrigan!" Radleigh and Trix scolded. "Answer Deputy Best!"

"Right. Sorry. I acted instinctively. I thought I was quite safe amidst a crowd of gala-goers, so I introduced myself and tried to glean as much information from Mr. Venn as possible."

"And what did you find out?" Charlie asked.

"Not much, unfortunately. He was rather cryptic in his replies to my questions."

Trixie asked, "Do you think he was the one who ransacked your place?"

"No, as he and I left at the same time. Marcia Wells and Julian left well before I did after I witnessed them in a heated discussion."

Charlie scribbled into his notebook. "Any idea what it was about?"

"None whatsoever. However, Julian was quite cool with Marcia the entire evening. I suspect it was due to their spat at the festival earlier today, which also involved Robert Grant."

"Was Mr. Grant at the gala?" Charlie asked.

"No, he wasn't. So, put him on the list of potentials for turning my house upside down." I pointed to Charlie's notepad. He scribbled Robert's name under the rest.

"You're sure you have no clue what they would be looking for?" Charlie asked.

I felt Radleigh and Trixie's eyes on me. "No clue whatsoever." I lied, fingers crossed behind my back. "I think Marcia Wells or Robert Grant would have the most to gain from Lydia's death, don't you, Charlie?"

Charlie closed his notepad. "It would appear so, but their alibi's checked out. Marcia was at a meeting in her Portland office, and Robert was at a real-estate conference."

"Oh. I see." So much for that theory. "But maybe they returned in time..."

Charlie shook his head. "They were both on the red-eye back to Castle Point that night. They couldn't have done it."

My stomach felt like a stone was firmly lodged in it. Just because Marcia and Robert weren't in Castle Point at the time of Lydia's murder doesn't mean they didn't kill Lydia. They could have hired someone. Victor Venn, perhaps. I suggested the same to Charlie.

He replied with his standard answer, which set my teeth on edge: "Leave the investigating up to the professionals, Miss Critt."

———

Once Charlie and his deputy finished up and left, I changed into sweats, and Trixie, Radleigh, and I straightened up.

After an hour of righting, cleaning, and fixing, my little house finally looked like a home again. With an accomplished sigh, Trixie eased onto the couch opposite me, tucking her legs beneath her. Her eyes flickered with concern and curiosity. She pulled an ever-ready crochet project from her bag, and I did the same. Radleigh poured us a glass of wine each and took the comfy chair closest to the fireplace.

"So, spill it. Why did you lie to Charlie about the formulas? Also, how was the rest of the gala? Were you the Bell of the Ball?"

"Oh, don't be ridiculous, Rad. You know you're the only 'Bell of the Ball' here or anywhere. I knew Charlie would confiscate the evidence, and I am not quite done with them yet."

Trixie's voice filled with concern. "Carrie, it's illegal to withhold evidence. You could get in so much trouble!"

I nodded. "I know, Trix. I'll figure out how to get them into Charlie's hands, but not yet."

With each double crochet stitch and sip of wine, I filled my compatriots in on the events of the evening.

I let my thoughts untangle like the yarn from its skein. "I can't shake this feeling that Victor is involved in Lydia's death. Otherwise, why would he have come into her store? And why did he run from us if he wasn't guilty of something? And why be so elusive this evening?"

"He just *had* to be rummaging her shop for the journals or the formulas, right? Maybe he and Marcia or Robert are working together?" Trixie offered, her crochet hook busy hooking away. Trixie was one amazing hooker.

The rhythmic thrum of metal against yarn was the only sound piercing the silence of my living room. "I think he was looking for the formulas, yes. But I don't think he's in cahoots with Marcia, as the two times I've seen them in the same vicinity, Marcia doesn't even acknowledge Victor's presence."

Radleigh nodded slowly, his gaze fixed on my hands as they worked. "He's a mysterious one, for sure. I'm leaning toward Marcia if I'm honest. She and Julian left the gala early, right?" he mused. "And I think she had the most to gain from Lydia's death, wouldn't you agree? Even Lydia's ghost has pointed fingers toward Marcia, right?"

"That's just it," I replied, frowning at my growing creation. "Lydia's so confused, she's barely able to recollect anything, and it's flummoxing me."

"Could be she's scared," Trixie offered, reaching for a stray ball of yarn and tossing it lightly between her hands.

I paused mid-stitch. "Scared? Lydia? She was gentle but also fierce—in life, that is." But Trixie had a point—death changes people... or ghosts.

"Carrigan, do you remember that kerfuffle between Marcia and Lydia at the festival?" Radleigh cocked an eyebrow, a spark igniting in his eyes.

My hook stopped mid-air as memories swirled back. "Yeah, that was quite the ruckus. Also circumstantial. We only heard about the argument through Eunice. Not what it was about."

Trixie leaned forward, elbows on knees. "Maybe Marcia didn't just borrow the idea for a botanical line... she stole it from Lydia. I'm with Rad on this one, Carrigan. Marcia had much more to gain from Lydia's death than anyone. Even Robert."

I shook my head. "You heard Charlie. They both have a solid alibi for Lydia's death."

Trixie stopped mid-stitch. "Well, yes, that's right. They were both in Portland."

"So, there's definitely a connection there! What do you think it could be?" Radleigh asked.

"I suppose it depends on what they were doing." The tension in my shoulders eased as the steady movement of my hands worked its calming magic on me. The crochet project was taking shape—a scarf, perhaps? It was hard to tell when thoughts were swirling faster than a tornado carrying farm animals.

"So, what do we do now?" Radleigh asked after a moment of comfortable silence.

I looked down at the red yarn unfurling from its center—red like alarm, urgency, passion—a color to wake the senses.

"We keep digging, starting with Marcia and Robert and their connection in Portland." I declared with newfound resolve. "We sift through every nook and cranny of gossip and scuttlebutt until we strike gold—or arsenic."

CHAPTER 13
GHOSTS & GRAVES

I WRAPPED another row of crimson loops around the crochet hook, the yarn a fiery contrast to the somber thoughts swirling in my head. A small mountain of discarded tea bags lay beside an empty bottle of wine, evidence of time's passage as I switched from wine to tea and wrestled with theories and tangled threads.

The scarf had taken on a life of its own, a textile serpent sprawled across the living room floor, weaving between furniture legs and over Trixie's slumbering form. She'd succumbed to the warmth of the room and the lull of my monotonous stitch count. I checked my watch. It was after three a.m.

I glanced at Radleigh sleeping in the armchair, his serene expression and a droplet of drool inching towards his chin. I stifled a chuckle. Even in sleep, their presence was a comfort.

I set down my hook and stretched, joints popping in protest. The scarf, now easily long enough to swaddle a small army, lay coiled at my feet. It was an impressive piece, if utterly impractical. I had let my hands busy themselves while my mind roamed.

The list of suspects in Lydia's journals still played

hopscotch in my brain. Marcia Wells, her public squabble with Lydia casting her in a sinister light; Robert Grant, his inheritance motives as clear as day; Julian and Liz and their connection with Marcia; and now, Victor Venn, that enigmatic figure who could be key to unraveling this rigmarole.

But where did all this lead? Each path I wandered down ended in a maze of maybes and what-ifs—a real hullabaloo that left me bumfuzzled.

With Trixie and Radleigh out cold and no further epiphanies knocking at my brain, I considered the merit of fresh air. A night stroll through Critt Memorial Gardens might offer clarity—or at least free me from the captivity of endless yarn.

I scribbled a note for my team in case they woke up bewildered by my absence, then tiptoed past them, snagging my jacket on the way out.

The cool night air hit me like a splash of reality as I locked up behind me. The town slept under a quilt of stars and secrets. My boots crunched on the gravel path leading to the gardens, each step echoing like a metronome for my thoughts.

Reaching the familiar wrought-iron gates, I traced their intricate patterns with my fingertips. Lydia's ghost had not revealed anything groundbreaking since our last encounter when she exposed her secret hiding place. Her spirit was probably just as frustrated as mine, if not more.

I considered walking to Lydia's shop—the place that had trapped her ghost since her demise—to speak with her, but I walked through the gardens first to gather my thoughts.

A gentle breeze stirred, sending leaves skittering across stone paths like spectral footsteps hurrying to some urgent midnight rendezvous. I strolled among tombstones and mausoleums that held fast to their secrets. They were reliable companions—silent but never judging.

My boots paused beside an angel statue, its stone wings forever poised for flight. The name plaque glinted in the moonlight; *"Caspian Critt. Father, Husband, Friend."* A sigh escaped me. "I wish you were here tonight, Dad. I wore a *gown* and went to a *gala.* Can you believe it?" I ran a hand down the angel's face. "You would have loved it. The music, the dancing...I *danced,* and I didn't even trip over my feet! Well, barely."

I sighed again—a mix of exasperation and resolve, my thoughts returning to the mystery of Lydia's death. There had to be something we missed—some nugget buried under layers of daily musings and tittle-tattle.

As I stood under the watchful gaze of the stone angel, my thoughts circled what I knew. Lydia's ghost had mentioned that VV wouldn't pay—blackmail? And VV and MW—Marcia Wells—desperate to reclaim... what? Something she believed Lydia stole from her? What if these weren't separate threads but strands of the same rope, and Marcia and Victor worked together?

My phone vibrated in my pocket, shattering my train of thought. I pulled it out to see a text from Charlie: "Arsenic found in the teacup–lab just confirmed."

I typed back a quick reply, thanking him for sharing the info. For some ungodly reason, my overtired and bumfuzzled brain followed that up with: *"Musical mud pies keeping you awake as well?"* Fiddlesticks. Damn, these uncoordinated bean-pole fingers I'd been cursed with. Why must they embarrass me so?

Charlie: *"I can't say I have ever encountered a musical mud pie, nor have thoughts of one kept me awake..."*
Me: *"Ha-ha, all thumbs tonight! I meant Murder Melodies."*
Me: *"Melancholies,"*
GOOD GRAVY!
Me: *"M Y S T E R I E S!"*
Charlie: *"Always, Miss Critt. Always."*

———

My pace quickened as I left Dad's gravesite and walked past shuttered shops and silent homes. I stopped at the back door of Lydia's shop and dug into my pocket, retrieving the key and the broken piece of barrette Alfie had found. Holding it up to the streetlight, I examined it—a jagged edge where it had snapped off, but a small pearl remained. It was a peculiar piece; few people wore barrettes these days except...

My breath hitched as an image of Liz flashed through my mind—Liz with her perfect hair, often clipped back with decorative barrettes.

A shiver raced down my spine as the pieces slotted into place. I slipped the key into the lock, opened the door, and slipped inside.

I flicked on the shop lights, the fluorescents sputtering to life with a reluctant buzz. The room greeted me like an old friend who had seen better days.

"Lydia?" My voice barely rose above a whisper, but it seemed to carry the weight of a scream in the shop's quiet. "Are you here?"

The air shifted subtly; a perfume of herbs and flowers whispered through the room. I turned toward her desk chair, and there she was—Lydia's ghost, hovering with a spectral grace that defied her tragic end.

"Carrie," she murmured, her voice as soft as the flutter of moth wings against a lampshade.

I took a cautious step closer. "Lydia, I've been thinking about everything you've told me—and what I've found out." I paused, collecting my thoughts like pebbles to lie out before her. "The cause of your death has been confirmed: arsenic in your teacup."

Her expression twisted in a blend of confusion and dawning horror. "Arsenic? But how? Who?"

"That's what I'm trying to figure out." I drew a breath and plunged on. "You mentioned possible blackmail—someone trying to use what you knew against you."

Lydia nodded slowly; her form shimmered as if this effort of memory strained even her ghostly existence. "Yes, I... I had something valuable. Something Marcia wanted back desperately."

I remembered the note cards with formulas scribbled across them—the same ones gracing Marcia's products. "The formulas that I found in the wall," I ventured, "they were what Marcia wanted?"

She gave a sorrowful nod, and her eyes met mine with a clarity that chilled me. "Yes. But they were evidence of the betrayal."

Betrayal—there was that word again. It tasted bitter on my tongue. Lydia had been playing a dangerous game—one that cost her life.

"Lydia," I pressed on gently, "Betrayal against who? In your journals, you mentioned VV - is that Victor Venn? Did he have anything to do with this?"

Her gaze wavered for a moment before steadying. "Victor... yes, Victor. He wanted those formulas, too." She sighed —a sound like wind through fall leaves.

"Did Victor know about Marcia's intentions?" I asked.

Lydia hesitated, then shook her head slowly. "I don't think so. They weren't allies—if that's what you're suggesting."

Allies or not, they were entangled in this web of secrets and ambition—a web that had snared Lydia fatally.

"What about Liz?" The question slipped out before I could stop it.

Lydia frowned slightly, puzzling over the name as if it were unfamiliar or distant. Her eyes widened slightly as recognition dawned.

"Liz," she whispered with an edge of suspicion. "She always asked too many questions about my work."

Questions that could lead to pilfering secrets? The broken barrette piece felt heavy in my pocket—was it a clue or a dead end?

I needed more from Lydia, but pushing too hard might scatter her thoughts like dandelion seeds on the wind.

"Lydia," I coaxed softly, "the night you died... can you remember anything? Anything at all?"

She closed her eyes—or perhaps it just seemed that way—and for a moment, there was only silence.

"I was working late," she began hesitantly. "There was someone at the door..."

My heart thumped against my ribs like it wanted out.

"The front door?" I prompted when she faltered.

"Yes..." Her form wavered again; frustration creased her brow. "Tea... I offered tea..."

The arsenic-laced tea—the cup confirmed by Charlie earlier tonight.

"Who did you offer tea to, Lydia? Who came by?"

But Lydia's face crumpled into confusion; the memory slipped through her grasp like water through clenched fingers.

"I... can't remember." Despair tinged her voice, and it pained me to see her so distraught.

"It's okay," I reassured her hastily, not wanting to lose our tenuous connection. I fetched the piece of barrette and held it up to her. "Lydia, Alfie found this piece of broken barrette in the floorboards of the shop. Does this belong to you?"

Lydia peered at the piece in my hand and shook her head. "I don't think so. I rarely wear hair clips of any kind. Or, at least, I didn't..." she bowed her head sadly.

The shop seemed to hold its breath, every creak and whisper amplified in the stillness. Lydia's spectral form flickered like a flame caught in a draft, and I knew my time with her was running out like sand in an hourglass.

"I'm so sorry for all the questions, Lydia. I know this must be painful for you. I need to ask about Robert and Julian Ravenscroft." I asked, trying to piece together the rest of the puzzle. "How do they fit into all of this?"

Lydia's expression darkened, a shadow passing over her ethereal features. "Robert," she began, her voice heavy with emotion. He wanted out—out of our marriage, out of the business...but "not without a parting gift from me."

The bitterness in her tone didn't surprise me; estrangement could turn toxic if left unchecked. "A parting gift? You mean your shop? The formulas?"

She nodded, a ripple disturbing her outline. "He suddenly felt entitled to what I'd built... which was confusing because his disinterest in my business had been glaringly obvious for years."

I frowned, thinking back on my conversation with Robert. His grief had seemed genuine, but grief could be a mask for guilt just as quickly. "Were you going to give him a divorce?"

Lydia paused, then slowly shook her head. "I was thinking about it, yes. But not until I knew my business would be protected..."

"And Julian?" I pressed on. "What's his role in Marcia's schemes?"

Lydia's face twisted into a wry smile. "Julian," she murmured, "he's always been Marcia's lapdog—eager to please for scraps from her table."

"So he was in cahoots with Marcia?" The idea wasn't far-fetched; lawyers and their clients often formed alliances thicker than thieves.

"Cahoots," she repeated with a faint laugh that held no joy. "Yes, you could say that. He protected her interests... aggressively."

Her words painted a picture of Julian that aligned with the smugness I'd sensed during our dance at the gala. But protecting interests was one thing; murder was another league entirely.

I hesitated, weighing my following words carefully. "Did either of them ever threaten you? Or show any sign that they might be... dangerous?"

Lydia floated closer, enveloping me like mist rolling off the ocean. "Threats are common in a competitive business like mine—especially when your success overshadows others." Her gaze drifted away, lost in some private recollection.

"But actual danger?" I pressed. "Could you imagine any of these people hurting you?"

She looked back at me, and there was sorrow in those ghostly eyes—sorrow and fear mingled together like bitter herbs in a brew.

"Everyone wears masks, Carrie," she breathed. "Some just hide sharper teeth behind theirs."

Her cryptic words settled over me like dew on morning grass—cool and unsettling. It wasn't enough to point fingers or cast accusations; Lydia's hints were as elusive as smoke.

"So, you're saying they're all capable of murder?" I concluded aloud.

She did not answer but hovered there with an air of resignation that tugged at my heartstrings.

I wanted to comfort her—to tell her we'd find justice—but the platitudes turned to ash on my tongue. Instead, I shifted gears.

"Lydia," I ventured gently, "can you try to remember anything else about the night you died? Anything could help us."

She closed her eyes again, and for a moment, her silence was as profound as the ocean's depths. "I'm sorry," she whispered, looking as distraught as I felt. Her form dissipated like fog under a rising sun.

"No, don't go!" The plea escaped me; desperation clawed at my throat.

Lydia's ghost lingered for a moment—a sad smile gracing her lips before she vanished entirely, leaving me alone amidst shadows and secrets once more.

I stood in the silence that followed—it roared in my ears

like a waterfall—and let out a long breath I hadn't realized I'd been holding.

The clues Lydia had provided were puzzle pieces that refused to fit together neatly; each revelation further complicated the picture. Robert's sense of entitlement to Lydia's success, Julian's protective ferocity over Marcia's interests, and, more importantly, Marcia and Victor wanting something Lydia had.

I turned off the shop lights and locked up behind me, my mind still churning with half-formed theories and elusive answers. The light of a new day whispered across the sea as I went home through the sleeping streets, forming questions in my mind—questions for Liz about her probing curiosity into Lydia's work and Victor about his reasons beyond revenge. And, for now, I'd have to ignore Robert and Marcia's alibis, as anyone with so much to gain from Lydia's death would indeed find a way…

Exhaustion clung to my bones, but there would be no time for a nap. Today was another day, a day for interviews and hopefully answers, bringing me one step closer to unmasking Lydia's killer.

CHAPTER 14
DEATH & DESPAIR

BACK AT THE HOUSE, Trixie stirred on the couch as I entered.

"Carrie?" she mumbled sleepily.

"I think I've got something," I said with more conviction than I felt.

Trixie sat up, rubbing her eyes. "What is it?"

I told her and Radleigh about my late-night convo with Lydia's ghost.

"Marcia and Robert had motive," Radleigh stated, rubbing the sleep from his eyes. "But what about their alibis?"

I walked into the kitchen to start the coffeemaker. Trixie and Radleigh followed. "I have to ignore them for now. I need to talk to Marcia again. Try to back her into a corner. Perhaps, if I mention the formulas and show her the cards, she'll confess…"

My phone buzzed: Charlie. "Sorry, guys. I gotta take this." I stepped away to answer his call while they discussed our next move.

"Charlie?" I answered.

"Carrigan, we've got a problem," he said without preamble.

"What kind of problem?"

"It's Marcia Wells."

"Oh, what about her?" I gripped the phone tighter.

"She's dead."

The room spun slightly as his words sunk in.

Marcia. Dead.

"Oh no. Do you know how...?" My voice barely rose above a whisper.

"Not confirmed yet—but I'm with my team at the festival grounds where it happened. From the pool of blood around her, my guess is a severe blow to the head. We'll need you down here to ...collect her corpse."

I glanced at Trixie and Radleigh; they looked back at me expectantly. "Charlie," I said with renewed purpose, "thanks for letting me know. I'll be there shortly."

The puzzle pieces that were aligning were suddenly smashed and lying in a heap of confusion on the floor of my mind.

———

The morning dew hadn't yet lifted from the grass, casting a surreal haze over the festival grounds as Alfie, Radleigh, Trixie, and I arrived, me pushing the gurney and Alfie riding on the top like furry royalty.

A gaggle of early birds fluttered around the crime scene tape, their whispers mocking the stillness of death.

The morning's somberness settled on my shoulders like a lead cloak as we stepped through the crowd, parting the onlookers with a firmness that surprised even me. The sun peeked shyly over the horizon, casting a sunny glow that felt inappropriate given the gravity of the situation.

"Miss Critt," a familiar voice cut through the chatter, pulling my gaze to Deputy Best. He stood there, tall and commanding, with his hands clasped behind his back.

"Charlie," I greeted, my voice steady despite my stomach churning. "I assume you've determined how Marcia met her end?"

His eyes, those deep pools of amber, held mine with an intensity that sent a shiver down my spine. "As I assumed. Blunt force trauma to the head," he said, his words clipped and efficient. "Seems our killer has a penchant for theatrics—first poison, now this."

I nodded, the pieces of this morbid puzzle swirling in my mind. "Are you assuming it is the same person who killed Lydia? Do you have any leads on what weapon was used? Or who might have wielded it?"

"We're not drawing conclusions just yet," he replied, his gaze drifting to the onlookers as if they might harbor secrets amidst their morning gossip. "The murder weapon hasn't turned up yet either."

"Alright." I swallowed hard, steeling myself for what came next. "If you're finished with the body, Radleigh and I will take her to the funeral home." The finality of those words never got easier.

Charlie's eyes softened slightly—a brief flicker of humanity in his stoic facade. He reached out a hand and grasped mine in a slight handshake that sent my tummy into a tumble. "Take care of her, Miss Critt."

I nodded before turning away from him and the scene that seemed to ripple with unanswered questions. "Let's go, Rad. Work to do." Radleigh nodded, pushing the gurney.

"What can I do?" Trixie asked.

"Perhaps mingle with the growing crowd and find out if anyone has any details–in the nicest way possible. I know the deputies are here but aren't the best at managing people's emotions."

"Will do," Trixie turned to greet several festival attendees.

As Radleigh and I approached Marcia's body, Alfie trailed

close behind us like a furry guardian angel. His presence was a comfort.

As I stood there, the chill of the morning dew seeping through my shoes, I glanced around, searching for any sign of Marcia's ghost. Spirits often lingered, especially when death came suddenly and violently, leaving them as dazed in the afterlife as we were in the wake of their passing. My skin prickled with the familiar sensation of a spectral presence, a shiver that ran deeper than the cold.

And there she was.

Marcia's ghost hovered inside the crowd of rubberneckers, her ethereal form flickering like a faulty neon sign. She looked as sharp-tongued and formidable as in life, yet there was a vulnerability in her translucent eyes that I'd never seen before.

"Marcia," I murmured under my breath, making sure not to draw attention to myself. Despite Castle Point residents' commonalities with witches and the supernatural, conversations with ghosts raised eyebrows. I could see Charlie peering at me out of the corner of my eye, and I suddenly felt ghost-shy.

Radleigh, noting my reaction, moved toward Marcia's body, calling Deputy Best's attention to assist.

Marcia's gaze snapped to mine, a silent storm brewing behind those spectral irises. "Carrigan Critt," she spat out my name like a curse. "Can you believe this?" her apparition said, pointing to her body. "Of all the ghastly indignities..."

I took a cautious step closer, aware of the police officers buzzing around us like bees to honey. "I'm sorry for what happened to you," I said, genuine despite our less-than-amicable history. Do you remember anything? Who did this?"

She floated higher, arms crossed over her chest in a gesture so quintessentially Marcia. It almost made me smile. Almost. "If I knew, don't you think I'd be screaming it from the rooftops rather than wasting my afterlife on chit-chat?"

Her voice dripped with sarcasm, but her frustration was palpable. I could feel it vibrating in the air between us. Her sharp tongue hadn't receded in death.

"Anything you can tell me could help," I pressed on, trying to keep my tone gentle yet firm. Ghosts were like skittish cats; too much eagerness and they'd vanish on you.

Marcia's form wavered, her face contorting as she tried to grasp onto memories that kept slipping through her fingers like sand. "It was all so... sudden," she said at last. "One moment I'm alive and well—the next..." She trailed off, shaking her head as though it could shake loose the recollection.

"Did you see anyone? Hear anything unusual?" I asked, trying to piece together what little she offered.

She released an exasperated sigh that seemed to ruffle the leaves on a nearby bush. "It's all bits and pieces," she confessed. "I heard footsteps—soft but deliberate—creeping up behind me."

I leaned in closer still, aware of Charlie's eyes occasionally flicking in our direction. "And then?"

"And then darkness," Marcia finished bitterly. "Whoever did this caught me unawares—a coward's move."

The words hung heavy between us, and for a moment, we stared at each other in anticipation.

"I wish I could give you more," she said after a pause that felt like an eternity.

"I understand," I replied softly. Death had a way of scrambling even the sharpest minds.

I took a deep breath and turned back to the scene unfolding around us—the officers documenting every inch of ground for evidence, Charlie conferring with his fellow deputies in hushed tones—too far away to catch any words.

I peered around, ensuring the local looky-loos were focused on the officers and not the tall, gawky mortician talking to a ghost. "Marcia, were you involved in Lydia's death?"

Marcia looked at me, frowning. "Lydia's death? Me? I had as little to do with Lydia as possible. Why would you think I was involved?"

"I know you were after something Lydia had. Her botanical formulas, for instance." I saw no point in being anything but blunt.

Marcia laughed. "Why would I want her botanical formulas? Anything that Liz and I created would have far out-shone Lydia's line. The idea that I killed her for–well–any reason is preposterous!"

"What about the other formulas?" I asked, referring to the note cards I'd found in Lydia's shop.

A howl from Alfie snapped my attention from Marcia's ghost before she could answer. A flash of something he was playing with beyond the scene caught my eye—a glint of something a few feet from where Marcia's body had lain.

Bending down under the pretense of tying my shoe, I saw a man's watch; the face busted and bloody, and half of the strap lay a few inches from the watch, as though it was ripped off and flung.

"Marcia?" I called to her quietly to avoid drawing attention to my position. Her ghost floated toward me. I grabbed a pencil from my bag and slid it through the buckle end of the watch, hoisting it up for closer inspection. "Any idea if this watch was worn by the person who hit you?"

Marcia peered at the watch. "I remember a blow to my head...nothing else..."

I grabbed my phone from my back pocket and snapped pictures of the watch. Behind the broken glass, the time stood still at 5:15. I wondered if that was perhaps Marcia's time of death.

"Marcia, do you recall what time you were struck?"

Marcia's expression was one of pure exasperation. "It's

not like I said, 'Wait, let me check the time before you kill me'! Good grief, Carrigan. I thought you were supposed to be good at this."

Ignoring her snarky reply, I rose and glanced over at Alfie, who sat patiently nearby. He seemed restless, his tail twitching with an energy that suggested he sensed something, too. "Charlie," I called out. "I found something,"

Charlie strode over to me, his brow furrowed. His eyes widened when he saw the shattered, bloody watch hanging off the end of my pencil. "Good work, Miss Critt. I'll take that." He smiled, reaching into his pocket for an evidence bag. I slipped the watch inside, hiding my delight at Charlie finally calling me by my first name.

"The time is frozen at 5:15. Think that's the time of death?" I asked, buoyed by the sight of his radiant white teeth.

Charlie gave a slight shrug. "I'll have to consult with the Coroner about that," he said. "You can take the body now, Miss Critt. We've got all we need from the scene," he said before walking off.

I rolled my eyes. Both at the brief first-name-basis interaction and somewhat doubting that he had gotten everything he needed from the scene, seeing as Alfie found the broken watch near Marcia's body.

The body lay still under the white sheet that did little to conceal the tragedy of what lay beneath. Contents from Marcia's belongings lay scattered beside her body, tagged with evidence markers. A flash from the deputy's camera glinted off something that caught my attention.

I stepped closer to the scattered contents and bent over.

There, amid lipstick and feminine hygiene products, was the vintage bottle of arsenic Marcia had shown me on the first day of the festival.

A flutter of ice-cold chills ran up and down my giraffe-like legs.

"Radleigh, look!" I said in a throaty whisper.

"What is it? What do you see?" he replied, peering at the contents.

"There." I discreetly pointed.

"I see three tampons and a maxi-pad," Radleigh replied, confused.

"No, silly. To the right of that."

The deputy who was photographing stepped away. When he did, I slipped my phone out of my pocket and snapped a few pictures myself, quickly tucking my phone away when I saw Charlie approaching.

"Need help with the body?" he asked.

I shook my head, my poker-straight hair whipping into my eyes. "All good here, Bestie," I said, saluting him awkwardly. Charlie shook his head and walked away.

With gentle hands, Radleigh and I transferred Marcia's body into a body bag and then onto the gurney.

Radleigh pushed the gurney ahead of me along the path, the wheels crunching over gravel, my mind a cacophony of thoughts and questions. Alfie trotted alongside; his feline senses alert to more than just the mundane world around us.

Marcia's ghost followed behind, her spectral form casting no shadow in the morning sun. She hovered near the oak tree that marked the entrance to the festival grounds, her arms folded in a familiar posture of defiance.

"You know," she said, her voice carrying a sharp edge even in death, "I had plans. Big plans."

I glanced over my shoulder, ensuring we were out of earshot from the living. "And did those plans have anything to do with the other formulas in Lydia's possession?"

Marcia scoffed. "You mean *my* formulas? You saw them?"

Radleigh stopped the gurney and turned toward me, his perfectly penciled eyebrows lifted.

"Give me a moment, will you, Rad? I have a few questions for Marcia."

Radleigh nodded, understanding that Marcia's ghost must

be in the vicinity. He played watchman in case the looky-loos got curious and came over.

"*Your* formulas?" I asked Marcia's apparition. "Lydia had *your* formulas?"

Marcia scoffed again. "Well, no, not mine, really. But the formulas she has, she stole from *me*." she folded her translucent arms defiantly. "I was trying to get them back from her before she was killed. If you ask me, she deserved it."

I shook my head, incensed. "Nobody deserves to be murdered, Marcia. Not even you."

Marcia's features softened. She bowed her head and wept ghostly tears. "I can't believe this has happened to me."

"I can imagine," I replied softly. "But sometimes fate has other ideas."

Marcia uselessly wiped at her face. Her raw emotion tugged at something deep within me. Sadness, anger, betrayal, and fear mingled into a bitter cocktail.

"So, you didn't kill Lydia."

Marcia stomped her feet. Another useless gesture. "Of course I didn't!"

I faced her fully, trying to offer what solace I could with my presence alone. "Okay, I believe you. Were you somehow involved with Robert Grant?"

Marcia paused. "Yes. Yes, I was."

"*How* were you two involved?"

"How do you mean?"

"Marcia, were you using Robert to get to the formulas Lydia had in her possession?"

Marcia merely looked at the ghostly space where her feet would otherwise have been.

Look, I know you're scared," I said, "and you have every right to be. But I need to know."

"I may have been using Robert...I'm not sure now..." Marcia's image blinked around the edges.

"Carrigan, people are watching…" Radleigh interrupted. "We need to go. Now."

I sighed and whispered to Marcia, "We'll find out who did this, Marcia."

Her expression softened for a moment before hardening once more. "You think comforting words will help?" she challenged, but there was less heat in her words now.

"It's not just words," I countered gently. "I have this… ability to help spirits like you find peace—closure, even."

Her laughter was hollow, echoing off the stone mausoleums with a chilling resonance. "Peace? Closure? And what do I get out of it? I'm still dead."

The bluntness of her statement hit me like a slap in the face—no amount of sugar-coating could change that stark reality.

"Yes," I admitted, meeting her gaze steadily. "But holding onto this anger won't change that either. It will only keep you tethered here, unable to move on from this… injustice."

For a long moment, Marcia said nothing; then she looked away from me and toward the rising sun, which bathed us in its golden light.

"I don't know how to let go," she confessed, her voice quieter now.

I moved closer until I could almost feel the cold emanating from her form. "Start by thinking about what mattered most to you," I suggested. "Focus on those memories—let them guide you."

She closed her eyes—a gesture more for thought than any need for rest—and took a deep breath that didn't stir the air.

"My business… my ambitions… they drove me," she began hesitantly. "But as well… Julian." Her face softened at his name.

"Think about Julian then," I urged gently. "Think about your happiest moments together."

A small smile played across Marcia's lips as she reminisced about something unseen.

"There was this one evening..." she trailed off but continued smiling.

"That's it," I encouraged. "Hold on to that feeling—that love."

Her form glowed softly as she embraced the memory fully—a warm light that grew brighter with each passing second.

Suddenly, she opened her eyes and fixed them on mine with an intensity that made my heart skip a beat.

"Thank you, Carrigan," she said; genuine gratitude in her tone now.

Then, with one last look at me and the world she was leaving behind, Marcia's light burst into a cascade of shimmering particles that rose into the sky and disappeared like stars fading at dawn.

A profound peacefulness enveloped me that seemed to affirm Marcia had finally found her way.

I let out a breath and turned back to my duty—transporting Marcia's remains to their final resting place before searching for justice on her behalf.

Radleigh brushed a tear from his face. "That was beautiful, Carrigan, helping her find peace..." he took out a deep purple handkerchief and blew his nose.

I smiled. "Meh. It's what I do. Now, let's get her body to the funeral home, shall we?"

CHAPTER 15
COFFEE & CROCHET

THE JOURNEY to Critt Family Funeral Home was a silent one, filled only with Alfie's soft purring, Radleigh's occasional sniffle, and the quiet hum of the engine.

Upon arrival at the familiar Victorian elegance, we transferred Marcia's body to the mortuary drawer, and I retreated to my office while Radleigh headed back to his apartment.

My thoughts were tumultuous as I sat at my desk, running through every interaction, every snippet of overheard conversation—anything that might lead me down the path to catching Marcia's killer.

With the discovery of the broken barrette and container of arsenic, my thoughts traced back to Marcia, potentially being Lydia's killer.

All evidence pointed to the possibility.

No. Probability.

But Marcia said she had nothing to do with Lydia's death.

The items could have just as easily been planted.

Alfie leaped onto my lap then, demanding attention with his insistent nuzzling. I nestled Alfie closer, his purring a steady thrum against the chaos of my thoughts. My mind buzzed with the potential why's and how's. The list of suspects tangled like the yarn Trixie loved to crochet into something beautiful.

Until now, a couple of paths led to Lydia's demise: Robert and Marcia. Both were obvious choices. But then, who ended Marcia's life?

Potentially, it was Robert Grant, whose estranged relationship with Lydia left him embittered—enough to kill? But what about Portland? He and Marcia had been there on the same night Lydia died. Julian Ravenscroft, her lover with his own set of secrets, was clearly upset with Marcia at the festival, then the gala, after perhaps finding out about her and Robert's affair–if that's what it truly was.

Victor Venn potentially harbored a grudge against both Marcia and Lydia potent enough to kill–but why? Where did he fit into the mix? And then there was Liz, her assistant, loyal but perhaps pushed too far? The missing lipstick gnawed at me like a mouse on cheese. It seemed too deliberate, too personal. Was it a message? A signature? Or a red herring meant to lead us astray?

One thing was certain; a killer—or killers—were still among us. The notion sent a shiver down my spine.

I let out a sigh, Alfie's weight grounding me. Alone, I could chase my tail for eternity and get nowhere. I contemplated taking a nap but was past the point of exhaustion. Grabbing my cell phone and clicking on the 'Hookers' group chat, my fingers flew across the screen. "Code yarn! Hookers assemble!" I paused, my stomach reminding me of my breakfast needs. "Meet me at the Chatterbox for breakfast!"

Radleigh's response came lickety-split: "On my way!"

Trixie chimed in seconds later: "Me too!"

Despite the gravity of our task ahead, a smile crept across my face. There was something comforting about their readiness to dive headlong into this kerfuffle with me. I gathered my notes, Lydia's note cards and diary and slipped them into my bag, along with a random ball of yarn and crochet hook sitting on my desk for such think-and-tinker emergencies. I glanced down at Alfie. "Hold the fort down, will you?" I said as he settled onto his cushion with feline disinterest.

————

I nudged open the door to the Chatterbox, the jingle of the bell announcing my arrival. The cafe, a symphony of clinking cups and soft murmurs, seemed more subdued than usual. I scanned the room for Eunice, finding her ensconced in her usual spot, a gossip queen upon her throne amidst the hum of the daily grind.

"Morning, Carrigan," she called out before I reached an empty table. She followed, pouring me a cup of coffee from a fresh, steaming pot before I could sit. "Heard about Marcia. Such a tragedy, huh?"

I slid into the booth, sighing. "Morning, Eunice. Yeah, it's a real calamity." I leaned in, lowering my voice to match the confidential tone that hung between us like a heavy stage curtain. Taking the hot cup of liquid energy in my hands, I took a long, satisfyingly hot gulp, willing my exhausted eyes to remain open.

Eunice perked up, her hearing aids practically sparkling with anticipation. "I bet you've got your hands full with all the going's on." She slid into the booth across from me and reached across the table, patting my hand with an artificial concern that didn't quite reach her eager eyes.

I couldn't help but chuckle. "You could say that," I admitted. "Seems like Marcia and Lydia are kicking up more ballyhoo dead than they ever did alive."

Her eyes widened, the red curls on her head bouncing as she nodded vigorously. "You know," she began conspiratorially, "I heard from a reliable source that Marcia and Julian were like two cats in a sack at the gala."

"I witnessed a few spurned moments as well, but was

distracted before I could find out more." My interest was piqued despite myself; Eunice always had the scuttlebutt before anyone else.

"Oh yes," she continued with relish. "Apparently there was some tittle-tattle about betrayals."

I frowned slightly; this tied into what Lydia's ghost had hinted at last night. It seemed like every corner I turned in this case revealed another cobwebbed nook of secrets.

I rubbed my temples where a headache was threatening to start its own hullabaloo. "Eunice, who do you think would benefit most from Marcia's death?"

She tilted her head thoughtfully, her chunky earrings swinging like pendulums. "Oh honey, I don't know Marcia personally, but from what I've heard through the festival vine, there's a list as long as my menu board…"

Her words rang true—a shiver traced its way down my spine as I considered the implications.

Just then, Trixie waltzed in with Radleigh in tow. She spotted us and waved energetically as they made their way over.

"Morning all!" Trixie chirped as they joined us at the table, pulling her latest crochet creation from her bag. Radleigh offered a gentle smile that didn't quite mask the concern etching his features.

"Trix, you are far too chipper for someone who spent half the night cleaning up my crime scene of a house, chatting and hooking," I said, rubbing my eyes.

"Agreed." Radleigh chimed in. "I barely had a moment to wash up and throw on something decent."

We both stared at him, flabbergasted, as he ran a perfectly polished hand through his perfectly quaffed and styled wig, before adjusting his gorgeous crocheted cardigan.

"Radleigh, you look runway ready, as always, while I'm sitting here looking like a Slavic Bag Lady. Don't give me any of that sass, mister." I said, with a look of amusement on my face.

"Oh, honey, I'm aware. But ya'll know I require at least thirteen compliments to start my day with a song and a smile." He replied with a wink.

Eunice clapped her hands together with excitement that bordered on ghoulish, given the circumstances. "Well! Our very own gang of crocheting crime solvers has arrived! This calls for some of my special blend—on the house." She stood up briskly and sauntered off to commandeer some coffees for us.

"Bring the entire pot, please Eunice!" I called out after her.

Trixie leaned forward eagerly as soon as Eunice was out of earshot. "Carrigan," she began in a hushed tone, "what do you think happened? You think Marcia's death is connected to Lydia?"

I glanced at Radleigh before responding, his face a mask of professional neutrality despite his bright scarf adding a pop of color to the otherwise dreary morning tableau.

"It's definitely more than coincidental," I admitted, running a hand through my hair in frustration. "Alfie found a broken watch near the body." I pulled out my phone and showed them the pictures I'd taken before handing the evidence off to Charlie.

"And Carrie spotted a bottle of that arsenic stuff in the contents of Marcia's purse," Radleigh said, his tone hushed.

Eunice returned then with our pot of coffee and cups, placing them down with an expectant look that begged to be included in our sleuthing circle. Our collective silence was a message received, and Eunice bussed the surrounding tables while remaining within the hearing-aide vicinity.

"Yes, I did. But Marcia's ghost said she had nothing to do with Lydia's death, so, if that's true, then finding those things has just become another part of the mystery." I took a welcome swig of coffee. "We'll need to figure out who owned the watch, and who this came from," I said resolutely, pulling the broken barrette out of my pocket.

"And we will," Radleigh assured me with fierce conviction.

We all sat there for a moment longer than necessary; sipping coffee, slipping a stitch, and contemplating our next move in silence.

"I can't shake this feeling," my voice was low. "The missing lipstick from Marcia's vintage collection—the same one found by Lydia's body—it has to be a key."

Trixie nodded slowly. "Can you really say for certain that Marcia is innocent? I mean, if you found the bottle of poison in her possession, then she must have had something to do with it, or it has to be someone trying to frame Marcia..."

Radleigh drummed his fingers on the table thoughtfully. "True. Or maybe she used the poison to off Lydia, but didn't count on being double-crossed before she could put it back on display?"

"But who would be cunning or desperate enough to turn on Marcia?" I mused aloud. "Marcia would have a lot to gain from Lydia's death if it were Lydia's formulas she was after, but when I asked her, she scoffed at the thought. She said that Lydia *stole* formulae from *her!* Also, there's Victor rummaging through Lydia's shop to consider. And there may be something to Marcia and Robert's alibis."

"We need to find out if they were together, at any time during that trip," Trixie whispered.

"It would make sense that they were," Radleigh added. "But how does Victor tie into all of this?"

A thread was emerging from this tangled skein that might lead us straight to the truth if we were careful not to pull too hard and unravel it all. I leaned back in our booth, feeling the weight of responsibility settle on me like an ill-fitting coat. This was about justice for two lives snuffed out too soon—and maybe preventing a third.

"We need more than speculation," I said finally, meeting their gazes individually. "We need proof."

The door chimed its merry jingle. Heads turned as Mother made her grand entrance, every eye drawn to her like moths to a flamboyant flame. My heart skedaddled up my throat at the sight of her.

"Mother," I groaned under my breath, bracing myself.

She floated toward us, her ensemble a riotous clash of avant-garde meets garden party. "Darlings!" she trilled, air-kissing each of us with the gusto of bestowing knighthoods.

"Mother," I said flatly. "We're kind of in the middle of something."

"Such fun!" She waved away my protest like an annoying fly. "I've found him, Carrigan!"

"Found who?" Radleigh asked, ever the peacemaker.

"*The one*!" She clasped her hands together as if in prayer or plotting—hard to tell with Mother.

Trixie's eyes lit up. "The one what?"

"The one! For Carrigan! His name is Victor Venn!" she announced as if she'd just revealed the secret bachelor behind door number three.

My jaw might've hit the floor if it wasn't already slack from shock. Trixie and Radleigh mirrored my disbelief; three statues frozen by this unexpected twist in our amateur investigation.

"Victor Venn?" I echoed, feeling a mix of annoyance and intrigue stir within me like a poorly mixed cocktail. "The genealogist?"

"The very same," Mother beamed, oblivious to our stunned silence. "He's dashing and sophisticated—"

"And possibly dangerous," I muttered.

She scoffed. "Carrigan, don't be dramatic."

"Dramatic?" Trixie piped up, regaining her voice. "Morgana, he's somehow tangled up in Lydia's murder!"

Mother blinked at us with an incredulous lift of her brows. "Murder? Our Victor?"

Radleigh dabbed at his lips with a napkin before chiming in gently. "Morgana dear, Victor's motives are murkier than a foggy night in Castle Point."

But Mother was undeterred; she perched on the edge of our booth with the confidence of a queen on her throne. "I'm sure it's all just some silly misunderstanding," she insisted.

"Or skullduggery," I said flatly.

She patted my hand patronizingly. "Carrigan, you've always had such an active imagination."

Trixie leaned forward. "Active imagination? Carrigan has been working this case with Char—"

My eyes darted to Trixie with a silent plea to not divulge too much about my ghostly informants or my chats with Charlie.

"Working... on this case. *Alone.*" I finished for Trixie, shooting her a look that said, *'Do not tell my mother I have been conversing with another man, or she will surely attempt to sell me off to the said man for three goats and a prize-winning hog.'*

"Well, then!" Mother stood up briskly. "You'll have plenty to talk about over dinner." She winked at me—a move that sent chills down my spine like an ill wind whispering through Critt Memorial Gardens at dusk.

"Dinner?" The word escaped me like a wayward spirit.

"Yes!" She clapped once for emphasis. "I'm going to arrange for you two to meet tonight at Le Frou Frou."

I choked on my coffee—a bit too dramatically—and fought for composure while wiping droplets from my blouse. Le Frou Frou was Castle Point's fanciest French restaurant; not the sort of place where you'd discuss potential murderers over Beef Wellington.

"Mother," I start, steadying my voice as best I can, "how on earth do you know Victor Venn?"

She leaned in as if about to disclose the location of the

Holy Grail. "Why, I used to purchase cosmetics from the Venn Family line!"

Trixie and Radleigh exchanged looks while I sat there, mouth agape.

"Cosmetics? Venn?" I stammered.

"Darling, before the fall of the Venn Cosmetics empire, they were the crème de la crème of beauty products. Their line was divine—I still have a tube of Venn lipstick. It's my little treasure—impossible to find anymore." Her tone carries a note of sadness reserved for lost loves.

Mother's name-dropping Venn Cosmetics had me gobsmacked. How did I not know?

She stood, smoothing her dress with delicate gold-adorned hands. "Anyway, must dash. Victor will expect you at Le Frou Frou tonight, Carrigan. I'm off to arrange it!" And with that, she flounced off like one of Radleigh's drag queen divas exiting stage left.

CHAPTER 16
BOMBS & BEAUTIES

THE CHATTERBOX CAFÉ seemed to hold its breath as Mother departed before resuming its regular cacophony. Radleigh let out a low whistle while Trixie shook her head.

I slumped against the booth's cushioned back, the name 'Victor Venn' ricocheting around my skull like a rogue pinball.

"Yeah, it's right here…" Trixie said slowly, scrolling the 'Google Oracle' as Trixie aptly named the Google search engine. "Venn Cosmetics…"

Radleigh tapped his chin thoughtfully. "I recall my mother saying something about the corporate giant going under, but I was just a baby. My love for lipstick and eyeshadow didn't hit until later in nursery school."

Radleigh's quip about his boyhood had been a welcome tension-breaker, eliciting a chuckle from Trixie and me until the gravity of our situation pressed down on us once again.

Trixie's fingers danced across her phone screen, the glow from her device casting an eerie light on her face. "The Wells-Venn rivalry is like something out of a Shakespearean drama."

Radleigh leaned in, peering over Trixie's shoulder. "Spill the tea, darling."

"Well," Trixie started, "the Venn family was huge in cosmetics back in the day. Like, *huge*. Their brand was synonymous with luxury and quality. But then came the Wells family—Marcia's ancestors—with their aggressive marketing and... shall we say... less scrupulous business tactics."

Radleigh gasped theatrically. "The scandal!"

Trixie nodded solemnly. "It says here that the Wells released a line of products remarkably similar to Venn's best-sellers, undercutting their prices drastically."

"Classic predatory pricing," I muttered under my breath.

"Exactly," Trixie confirms. "It wasn't long before Venn Cosmetics crumbled. The final nail in the coffin was when their flagship product was recalled because of a 'manufacturing error.' Sales plummeted, confidence was lost, and lawsuits piled up like confetti after a parade."

Radleigh grimaced. "That must've been devastating for little Victor."

"And that's not all," Trixie added, scrolling further. "There were rumors of corporate espionage. Someone inside Venn Cosmetics leaked trade secrets to the Wells. A mole in their midst who sold them out for a pretty penny."

"Betrayal!" Radleigh clutched his chest as if struck by an invisible dagger.

There was that word again.

I tapped my fingers on the table, pondering this twisted tale of vengeance and vanity. "So, Victor grows up watching his family's empire turn to dust because of the Wells. If that doesn't sow seeds for a vendetta, I don't know what does."

"But why come after Lydia?" Radleigh wondered aloud.

"It has to be because she had something he wanted... or needed," I recalled Lydia's journals—the initials VV scrawled next to cryptic notes about blackmail and theft.

Trixie raised an eyebrow. "The formulas? The ones

Marcia's family allegedly pilfered from his? You think *those* are the formulas you found in Lydia's shop?"

"It's possible." I leaned forward, elbows on the table. "Marcia's ghost said Lydia had stolen *her* formulas. What if Lydia got her hands on the Venn formulas somehow—through Marcia, I'm assuming—and Victor found out?"

Radleigh drummed his fingers against his lips thoughtfully. "But then Marcia ends up dead, too," he pointed out.

A chill skittered down my spine as I considered that wrinkle in our cozy little mystery quilt. "Victor breaking into Lydia's shop makes perfect sense. He was searching for those formulas. But that doesn't prove he killed Lydia. Or perhaps he did, and Marcia caught wind of his plan and tried to stop him–got in the way."

Trixie looked between us, her eyes wide with realization. "Motive! If Victor reclaimed those formulas, he could've restored his family name—"

"—and ruined Marcia's legacy in one fell swoop," I finished for her.

Silence descended upon our little huddle as we let this theory marinate. Each piece seemed to fit together with an almost eerie precision, but I couldn't shake the feeling that we were missing something—a detail as tiny yet vital as a single thread holding together a tapestry.

"So, we have tons of motive on Victor–great. But where does Julian Ravenscroft fit into all this?" I asked out loud. My mind raced back to the gala—how Julian danced around my questions with all the grace of a seasoned fox trotter. Something about him didn't sit right with me.

Trixie tilted her head in contemplation. "He was always by Marcia's side... maybe he knows more than he lets on."

Julian—Marcia's lapdog—her lawyer... could he have somehow been Victor's way into Marcia's world?

"We need more information on Victor," I said, breaking the stillness that enveloped us like fog over a graveyard.

Trixie nodded in agreement while Radleigh sighed deeply, running a hand through his vibrantly colored hair.

"Let's boogie on out of here and get our Nancy Drew on." Radleigh slid from the booth.

As we gathered our things and prepared to leave, Eunice Pembleton's voice cut through the chatter of her bustling cafe like a bell tolling for attention.

"Vivian Vincent! Your latte and scone are ready!"

The three of us froze mid-stride, turning as one to see Liz —Marcia Wells' assistant—rise from her table near the window.

My heart hammered against my ribs as I watched her move toward the counter, her face calm and unassuming.

Radleigh whispered, his voice barely audible above the hum of surrounding conversation. "Did she just say, Vivian Vincent? As in…VV?"

Trixie's mouth hung open slightly in shock. "But she's Liz… Liz Vincent."

My mind raced, replaying every interaction I'd had with Liz since Lydia's death—her seemingly genuine shock, her plausible alibis, her professional demeanor—all possibly a façade for something much more sinister.

Eunice handed Liz a steaming cup and a small bag with her usual efficiency. "Here you go, dear," she said warmly.

Liz nodded her thanks and returned Eunice's smile before returning to her table.

We watched in stunned silence as she gathered her belongings—a notebook tucked under one arm—and left the cafe without so much as a glance in our direction.

Once she was gone, Radleigh exhaled sharply. "Well... that just turned our little shin-dig into a full-blown ho-down."

Trixie turned to me, brow furrowed in thought. "Do you think she could be VV?"

"Only one way to find out."

I gathered my thoughts as we rushed toward Liz, strolling

along the quaint cobblestone walkway toward the festival, the thrum of music and laughter growing louder with each step.

"Liz," I called out, catching my breath, my curiosity bubbling up like a cauldron on to boil.

Liz stopped and turned toward us, a smile dancing on her lips. "Hello, Carrigan."

"We heard Eunice call you 'Vivian' back at the Chatterbox?"

Liz continued to walk alongside us and chuckled. "Oh, that's me," she said with a dismissive wave of her hand. "Vivian's my first name. But people always call me 'Liz', the short form of my middle name, Elizabeth."

The revelation sent a tingle down my spine—pieces of an intricate puzzle were snapping into place.

"Vivian always felt so formal, so... old-fashioned." Liz continued. "Liz is punchier, wouldn't you agree?"

Radleigh hummed in agreement, his nod an exclamation point to Liz's statement. "Darlin', you could go by 'Muddy Waters' and still be fabulous," he winked.

My stomach knotted as we walked closer to the heart of the festival, the sounds of merriment an odd backdrop to the conversation I was about to have with Liz. "Did you hear about Marcia?" I asked, keeping my tone neutral despite the unease threading through me. I assumed she hadn't, or she wouldn't have been so casually sipping a latte now.

Liz stopped and turned to me, her brows knitting together in a delicate expression of confusion. "Hear what about Marcia?"

I glanced at Trixie and Radleigh. The look in their eyes urged me to continue. "She was found dead early this morning. Murdered." I said softly, bracing for Liz's reaction.

The coffee cup slipped from Liz's fingers, frothy cream splattering across the cobblestones. Her face drained of color, and she staggered back as if I'd struck her. "What?" she gasped, a hand flying to her mouth. "I had no idea. I...I was heading to the festival now..."

People around us cast curious glances at the commotion, but they were soon swallowed up by the bustling crowd and forgotten. My eyes stayed locked on Liz as she crumpled onto a nearby bench, her body shaking with sobs that seemed to wrench from deep within.

Radleigh rushed to her side with a tenderness I'd often seen. "Oh, honey," he cooed, placing a comforting arm around her shoulders.

I waited for Liz to gather herself before asking my next question. "I'm so sorry to ask this, but where were you early this morning?" The words felt heavy on my tongue, laden with implications I wasn't sure I wanted to explore.

Liz replied through tear-streaked cheeks and quivering lips, "I was at my hotel..." Her voice broke over the words like waves against a lonely shore.

Watching her distress, my gut twisted in an odd dance of skepticism and empathy. She seemed genuinely distraught— so much so that it smoothed over any immediate doubts that crept into my mind.

"I believe you," I said after a moment's pause, surprised at how readily the words came out. But something about her raw emotion made it hard not to. The fact of the matter remained—I would have to check her alibi with the hotel staff.

Liz lifted her head, eyes brimming with gratitude and something else—fear? Relief? It was hard to pin down. She clutched Radleigh's hand like a lifeline. "Thank you," she whispered hoarsely. "I just can't believe...she's gone. Murdered? Oh, my God."

The moment hung between us—a fragile bubble threatening to burst with the slightest prod. We let the silence settle around until Liz's sobs subsided into quiet sniffles. Radleigh offered her his handkerchief with an encouraging smile while Trixie patted her back.

As I watched them comfort Liz, part of me wanted to join in—to wrap an arm around her and tell her everything would be alright. But another part held back, rooted in place by an investigator's caution and the weight of unanswered questions. A nagging voice reminded me that tears could be as deceptive as smiles.

Liz composed herself as she wiped away the last remnants of her tears with Radleigh's lacy handkerchief. "I had several calls from an unknown number this morning," she mentioned, tucking a loose strand of hair behind her ear. "I thought it was a prank or scam caller, but more likely, the police were trying to contact me about Marcia."

With shaky fingers, she checked her phone. "Oh, there are messages," she said, tapping the voicemail button and listened to several messages from a familiar voice—Charlie Best—requesting to talk to her.

I felt a flicker of unease at the mention of the police and hearing Charlie's voice in particular. The idea of Liz and Charlie interacting set my teeth on edge, though I couldn't pinpoint why.

"I should head to the police department to talk to Deputy Best," she concluded, rising from the bench with a determination that seemed to steel her slender frame.

"Would you like us to come with you?" Trixie offered, her voice soft and concerned.

Liz shook her head, a wry smile tugging at her lips. "Thanks, but it's unnecessary."

Radleigh patted her back, his smile supportive but tinged with worry. "If you need anything—anything at all—you just holler, okay?"

Liz nodded and squared her shoulders. "Will do."

As she walked away, Trixie turned to me with furrowed brows. "Do you think she'll be alright?"

"More importantly, do you think she's telling the truth?" I asked.

Radleigh let out a low whistle. "I've seen and done some pretty amazing acting in my day. If this was a performance, it takes the prize."

I watched Liz's retreating figure blend into the festival crowd, her poise as perfect as a pageant queen. "She's tougher than she looks. The question is, is she tough enough to commit murder?"

CHAPTER 17
ALIBIS & AFFAIRS

A CLOAK of mid-morning sun wrapped around us as we strode toward the festival management booth, the air thick with the aroma of fried dough and spun sugar. The crowd's chatter blended into a cacophony, almost drowning out the haunting questions that buzzed like hornets in my mind.

"I need to chat with Victor Venn again," I said with resolve. Mother had arranged a dinner date with Victor, which I would have to attend, much to my curiosity and dismay. "And Julian and Robert won't escape another round of questioning, either."

Trixie patted my arm. "What's your gut telling you?"

"That we're dancing around the edge of something deep." I squinted into the distance, where vendors hawked their wares and children laughed on rides that spun them through dizzying heights. "And I've got a feeling the men in Marcia's life are hiding more than just family secrets."

I left Radleigh and Trixie in charge of the festival and picked up Alfie. He purred in the passenger seat of the hearse, his whiskers twitching with every bump in the road as we made our way to Robert Grant's place. The idea of interrogating a widower about his late wife's rival—and now, corpse number two—sat in my stomach like a lead balloon.

Robert and Lydia's stately home loomed ahead, a relic of better times. I pulled into the driveway, noting the curtains drawn tight across every window. A shield against prying eyes, or perhaps the sunlight that might reveal too much dust in the corners of an unraveling life.

Alfie hopped out as I opened the door, darting up the path as if he owned it. I rapped on the front door, its solid oak a stoic barrier from the outside world. A moment passed, then two. The silence stretched long enough for me to consider leaving, but then footsteps approached, slow and heavy.

Robert Grant opened the door, his face a mask of grief, his eyes red-rimmed and puffy.

"Miss Critt," he greeted, his voice gravelly with emotion. "Please, come in." He moved aside with a heaviness in his step.

The house felt different from my last visit—the cool autumn air clung deftly to the walls. Alfie trotted beside me as I followed Robert into the parlor.

I glanced around the room, searching for Robert's all-too-friendly bird, and was relieved not to find him perched high on the bookcases. Alfie sniffed a random feather and meowed a warning.

Robert offered me a seat on one of the brocade sofas. I sat down gingerly, aware of my bulk against such delicate furnishings.

"Thank you for seeing me," I began. My voice sounded foreign in this museum of a home. "I'm sure you've heard about Marcia Wells?"

He nodded slowly, perching on the edge of an armchair across from me. "Marcia's death—it's a shock." His voice wavered before he cleared his throat and regained control.

I studied him. The line between genuine sorrow and skilled performance blurred under my gaze. Alfie chose that moment to leap onto Robert's lap, sniffed, and meowed loudly in Robert's face, forcing a startled laugh from him. Alfie looked at me before jumping down and surveying the rest of the room.

"Robert," I ventured, "Forgive me for asking, but were you and Marcia more than just acquaintances?"

He paused, his fingers still lost in Alfie's fur. His eyes met mine, and they were oceans of regret. "Yes," he admitted, his voice barely above a whisper. "We were having an affair. It started about a year ago."

The confession hung between us, heavy with implications. A year—that was no brief fling; it was a commitment of sorts.

"Was your affair the reason for your estrangement from Lydia?" The question slipped out before I could catch it.

"No, no, it wasn't."

"Why?" I wasn't sure if I was asking why he had an affair or why it *wasn't* the reason for the estrangement.

Robert's gaze dropped to his lap. "I suppose I was looking for something... someone to understand what I was going through with Lydia. Marcia... she listened." He shrugged as if trying to shake off the weight of his own words.

"You loved her." The statement hung between us like an uninvited ghost at a seance.

"Yes," he admitted after a pause. "I did."

"And Lydia? Did she know?" The investigator in me needed every detail; the human in me dreaded his answer.

His nod was slow, reluctant. "She found out several months ago." He glanced up again, his eyes stormy with memories best left untouched. "Even though we were already sleeping in separate rooms, having separate lives…the affair caused quite the rift between us."

"Did you still love her—Lydia, I mean?" The words felt intrusive even as they tumbled out.

Robert looked away, his expression unreadable for a moment before he turned back to me with something that resembled, resolve. "I thought I did," he said. "But love isn't supposed to hurt people like we hurt each other."

The raw honesty in his voice made me believe that beneath the mistakes and missteps; there might still be a decent man trying to find his way back to himself.

"Robert, I witnessed an argument between you, Marcia, and Julian Ravenscroft at the festival. Can you tell me what that was about?"

Robert practically barked at me. "I don't want to talk about it!"

Oopsie. Hit a sore spot. "Okay…Did Marcia say she had plans to meet someone this morning? Perhaps Julian?" I continued, pressing for details.

He shook his head. "We hadn't spoken in a couple of days. She was... preoccupied with her work lately."

"So, you haven't spoken to her since your argument at the festival."

"I told you, I don't want to talk about that!" he jumped up from his seat and paced the room.

"I'm sorry to upset you, Robert. I can't imagine how you must feel, losing Lydia and Marcia…" I said softly, reaching for empathy over suspicion. "But I need to ask you a couple more questions, then I'll be off, I promise."

Robert stopped pacing and met my eyes. "Fine," he replied tersely.

"Where were you early this morning?" I asked.

"At home," he answered without hesitation. "Alone."

No alibi, then—just his word.

"And you didn't hear from Marcia during the night? No calls or messages?" My tone stayed even though my mind raced with possibilities.

He shook his head—a simple gesture laden with finality. "Nothing."

"Robert," I leaned forward slightly, hoping my sincerity

would shine through. "If there's anything else you can tell me, it might help me find who did this."

He studied me for a long moment before sighing deeply, resignation etched into every line on his face. "I'll let you know if anything comes to mind," he offered, walking toward the door.

I nodded and rose, feeling the need to put some distance between myself and the palpable sorrow of this house. As I moved toward the door, I paused. Reaching into my pocket, I produced the broken barrette and showed it to Robert. "I found this in Lydia's shop. Any idea who's barrette this belonged to?"

Robert picked up the bit of plastic from my hand and squinted. "Can't say that I do. Sorry."

"Oh, not a problem. Just asking." I turned to the door, stuffing the plastic bit back into my pocket. "I won't take up any more of your time," I said gently.

"Thank you for coming by," Robert was stoic as he reached past me and opened the door.

"Oh. Silly me. One more thing," I said, turning toward him. "Have you got the time?"

He paused for a millisecond. "I'm afraid I've misplaced my watch," he said as he pulled his sweater up slightly, revealing a blank space amidst a tan line where a watch had been.

"Not a problem. Thank you." I murmured as Robert watched me silently.

I slid into my car with Alfie now purring in the seat beside me—a tiny engine revving up for no particular journey—and headed toward the Ravenscroft estate with more questions than answers knotting up inside my head.

———

The Ravenscroft estate loomed over the craggy coastline, its windows like eyes watching over Castle Point. Alfie pawed at

Julian's door, his meows rising to a fevered pitch. I couldn't blame him for his impatience; we were about to face Marcia's lawyer and lover, and I wanted the interview to be over with as much as Alfie did. I smoothed my blazer, steeling myself for the encounter.

I rapped sharply on the polished oak door, my heart matching each knock with a nervous thump. The door creaked open, revealing Julian's disheveled form. His usually immaculate hair was tangled, and his suit was crumpled like discarded paper.

"Julian," I started, "I heard about Marcia."

He motioned me inside with a weak wave of his hand. "Carrigan, I—"

His voice broke, trailing off into the grand foyer that echoed with silence as thick as fog.

I followed him into the living room, where every surface gleamed. Julian sank into an armchair, his face a mask of grief.

"Marcia was... She was everything to me," he whispered.

I perched on the edge of the sofa across from him, Alfie leaping up beside me to curl into a vigilant ball.

"Julian," I said softly but firmly, "I need to tell you something."

He looked up, eyes glassy but wary.

"It's about Marcia and Robert Grant," I continued. "They were having an affair."

Julian's expression shifted minutely—a twitch at the corner of his mouth—before he composed himself.

"I wasn't aware," he replied flatly and far too quickly.

His fleeting features screamed deception louder than wailing banshees. His jaw clenched slightly as he spoke; his hands tightened into fists before relaxing again. A shiver danced down my spine—I knew a lie when I saw one.

"You didn't? Are you sure? You realize that if you're

lying…that makes you suspect," I pressed on, ignoring Alfie's low warning growl.

"I told you, Carrigan," Julian cut in sharply, "I had no idea."

I leaned forward, my gaze never leaving his face, which seemed to etch deeper lines by the second.

"Julian," I said in a tone that brooked no argument, "if there's anything you're holding back, now's the time to share it."

"I have nothing to hide," he insisted.

I took a deep breath. "Julian, I saw you with Marcia at the festival the other day. You were arguing with Marcia and Robert Grant. Then, when I saw the two of you at the gala, you could barely look in Marcia's direction. What were you arguing about if it wasn't about Robert Grant?"

He rose abruptly from his chair and paced before the cold fireplace.

"Something entirely different," he muttered, more to himself than to me. "I'm telling you, I didn't know about her and Robert."

His denial hung between us like a cobweb—fragile and easy to tear through with just a touch of truth.

"Not until the confrontation at the festival. Isn't that right, Julian? Admit it!"

He huffed out a breath. Running a hand through his hair, he nodded. "Yes, fine. I didn't know about her and Robert until that day at the festival. You're right. But I didn't kill her!"

Satisfied with his answer–for now–I pressed on.

"Alfie found something at Lydia's shop." I watched Julian closely as I spoke. "A piece of plastic from what looks like a barrette."

Julian stopped pacing and fixed me with an intense stare that could've stopped a clock. He reached out to grab the broken piece. As he did so, a glaring piece of evidence caught my eye. A bit of untanned skin poked out beneath his tailored shirt—the size and shape of a watch face and strap—a stark contrast from Julian's noticeable "Florida" tan.

"What does that have to do with anything?"

"Just wondering if you've ever seen Marcia wear something like it." My words were casual, but my scrutiny was anything but.

He hesitated for a fraction too long before answering. "A plastic barrette? I doubt it. Marcia preferred more... sophisticated accessories."

My instincts were in overdrive; there was more to this story than Julian revealed. But pressing him further might drive him into silence—or worse—into actions born out of desperation. I took a deep breath and leaned against the plush cushions, watching as he resumed pacing. His movements were erratic, like a marionette with tangled strings—controlled yet somehow disjointed.

"You loved Marcia deeply," I said softly, breaking the silence that had settled over us like dust in an abandoned room.

He stopped mid-stride and turned to face me. "More than you could understand," he replied, his voice tight with emotion.

Alfie's ears twitched at Julian's tone, and he let out a low growl, a rumble of protective warning that vibrated through the silence.

I placed a calming hand on Alfie's head. "Love can make us do things we never thought possible."

Julian's eyes darkened, and he swiftly crossed the room until he stood before me. His presence loomed like an approaching storm cloud—intimidating yet somehow electric.

"I did not kill her! I did nothing but love her!" he declared, each word punctuated with a hint of defiance.

The air between us crackled. His declaration felt like a challenge—one I wasn't sure I wanted to accept.

"I'd like to believe you, Julian," I forced myself to meet his gaze. "But love can blind us to the truth and make us do the unfathomable."

He flinched at that as if my words had struck closer to home than he cared to admit.

"I'm sorry, Julian. I want to find out who did this," I said instead, my voice steady despite the chaos within me.

Julian's expression softened slightly at my words. "So do I," he whispered. "Is there anything else you need to ask me? If not, I'll see you out. I'm suddenly not in the mood for visitors."

I nodded slowly, feigning acceptance. "Of course," I murmured, keeping my voice light while my brain churned with suspicion.

Alfie mewed, leaped off the couch, and hurriedly headed for the door.

"Thank you for your time," I said at last, rising from my seat to follow Alfie. "You know where to find me if you remember anything else. I expect you will hear from Deputy Best shortly."

Julian escorted me out with a stiff courtesy that bordered on hostility. The door closed behind me with a thud.

As Alfie and I walked away from the house, my mind raced through everything Julian had and hadn't said.

His grief seemed genuine enough; it clawed at him visibly like thorns on delicate skin. But underneath it all lurked something else—a knowledge or guilt that didn't sit right with me.

I pointed the hearse toward home. It was time to prepare for my so-called 'date' with Victor Venn.

CHAPTER 18
UNDER-WIRE & URGENCY

AS I STOOD in the doorway of Le Frou Frou, my heart hammered like a drum-line in my chest, but I had to face Victor Venn. This man, with his vendetta as thick as the foundation on the face of Radleigh's drag-queen alter-ego, could be the linchpin to unraveling Lydia and Marcia's murders.

I spotted him at a table near the back of the quaint French restaurant. Taking a deep breath, I strode toward him, determined to unearth the truth buried beneath layers of deceit and betrayal. "Victor?" My voice came out steadier than I felt.

He turned, his eyes sharp and calculating. "Miss Critt," he acknowledged with a curt nod, standing and pulling out my chair. "Lovely to see you again," he said as he sat. I was pretty surprised when your mother called. She said you wanted to see me. Something about Marcia Wells."

I groaned, momentarily closing my eyes.

So, Mother didn't set this up as an actual date. How exasperating.

I put on a bra and pantyhose for nothing.

On the other hand, I had agreed to this arranged meeting because it offered me an excuse to question Victor. Perhaps

Mother's ulterior motives and bullheaded pushiness would benefit me for once.

Ignoring my continued annoyance at having to don underwire for the evening, I cut to the chase. "Victor, I know about the formulas—how Marcia Wells took them from your family, bankrupting you, and Lydia Grant was trying to sell them back to you." My assumption hung between us. I hoped being direct would throw him off a little–force him to provide some answers.

I was right.

For a moment, Victor's mask slipped, revealing a flicker of raw pain before he composed himself. "Yes," he hissed. "My family's legacy was stolen, and the Wells family's greed turned our lives inside out. But what does that have to do with me now?"

"Marcia Wells and Lydia Grant are both dead, Victor," I pressed on, locking eyes with him. "And both deaths revolve around those stolen secrets."

Victor sighed and leaned against the table, his fingers tracing the wood grain. "That's very unfortunate, Miss Critt," he began in an almost conciliatory tone. "I hadn't heard about Marcia Wells's demise. However, you've been led on a wild goose chase if you think I had any part in those women's untimely deaths."

"So, you deny your involvement? I'm sorry, Victor, but all roads lead to you…"

I braced for another round of denials or some flimflam designed to send me skedaddling off in the wrong direction. But Victor pulled out his phone and scrolled through it with deliberate swipes.

"Here," he said, turning the screen toward me. "This is my alibi for Lydia's death—my ticket to a genealogy conference I attended in Portland, and," he swiped through to another screen, "the log of my phone conversation with a colleague from Australia this morning. Early morning for me, late evening for Australia." The tickets, hotel receipt, and call log left no room for doubt; Victor was occupied when Lydia and Marcia met their fates.

My brain attempted to process this new information while keeping up appearances. I nodded slowly. "Alright then," I conceded, even as disappointment gnawed at me like a hungry rat. I would have to confirm his alibi, but I could eliminate him as a suspect if he were telling the truth.

Victor straightened up and fixed me with a look of pity and challenge. "Carrigan Critt," he said formally, "I am indeed seeking retribution for what the Wells did to my family. But not through murder." He paused before adding, "And not without proof."

My curiosity was piqued despite myself. "Proof?" I echoed.

"The original formulas," Victor clarified with a resolute nod. "The ones Lydia planned to sell me before she was killed." He crossed his arms over his chest as if shielding himself from further scrutiny—or perhaps protecting something even more valuable than his pride.

"So you haven't seen the formulas?" I prodded.

Victor shook his head. "No," he admitted ruefully. "It seems someone else got to them first."

We stood there for an awkward beat as I glanced down at my bag, the formulas tucked neatly inside.

I slid my hand into my sweater pocket and pulled out the broken barrette. "Do you have any idea who owned this?"

Victor peered at the piece and raised an eyebrow. "What an odd question. No, I would have no idea."

I slipped the piece back into my pocket. "Here's another odd question for you," I said. Victor leaned in closer. "Have you got the time?"

Victor scoffed and slid his jacket off his wrist. "It's 7:15 pm precisely."

I thanked him for his time and left just as the server came

to take our order, feeling like I'd just hopped off an emotional roller coaster only to land on a carousel spinning out of control.

But there was no time for dillydallying; I squared my shoulders. An idea popped into my head, and pieces of the puzzle slipped into place.

It was time to gather the guilty until proven innocent.

———

I perched on the edge of my well-worn sofa, hook in hand, red yarn unraveling from a skein like a truth waiting to be un-spooled. In walked Trixie, arms laden with skeins of crimson yarn, and Radleigh, arms laden with expensive wine bottles and chocolate bars. I'd texted the Hookers on my way home from the restaurant for a 'Think and Tinker' session.

And by tinker, I mean crochet.

Because, sometimes, you have to stitch your thoughts together before they make any sense.

Trixie sat across from me, crochet project in hand and curiosity on her face.

"They're all lying," I announced as soon as Radleigh joined us.

Radleigh perched on the edge of his seat like a gargoyle guarding sacred ground. "And what makes you think that?"

"It was as much about what each of them said as how they said it." My fingers tapped an impatient rhythm on the table's surface. "Every denial was too quick, too rehearsed."

Radleigh nodded slowly. "So, what's our next move?"

"We keep digging," I replied firmly.

The formula cards held the answers; Lydia had something Marcia and Victor Venn wanted. Were they worth killing for? The revelation of Liz's full name—Vivian Vincent—clung to my bones, adding weight to every hypothesis we'd tossed around. We needed answers fast before anyone else fell victim to this vicious vendetta.

"Think about it," I said, my fingers working the yarn into a pattern as my mind attempted to untangle the mystery. "The argument at the festival. Robert and Julian's faces were storm clouds ready to burst. They had just found out about each other."

Radleigh leaned forward, his expression intense. "So, you think Marcia was playing them both?"

"Yes." I nodded, grateful for his quick grasp of the situation. "Marcia had all her bases covered. Likely, she was truly in love with Julian, but she was with Robert for one reason: to get closer to Lydia and find the formulas. She kept the affair with Robert secret from Julian for months. Her mistake was being seen in public with either of them. She underestimated their reaction."

Trixie's eyes widened as she absorbed the implications. "So when they confronted each other in front of everyone..."

"They were squaring off over Marcia," I finished for her, "and possibly control over the formulas in Lydia's possession."

The silence that followed was thick with contemplation. I felt Alfie rub against my leg, his purring a soothing background to our brainstorming session.

"I still can't believe Liz is Vivian Vincent," Trixie muttered, breaking the silence.

"Yeah, what are the odds?" Radleigh added, disbelief coloring his tone.

"The same odds as me inheriting ghost-whispering abilities at forty," I quipped, drawing chuckles from both. "Marcia was caught in a web of deception," I mused aloud. "And it unraveled when Robert and Julian found out about each other."

"And one of them could have snapped," Trixie suggested, her voice laced with unease.

"Precisely." My hands faltered in their crocheting as I considered the possibility. "Robert seemed genuinely shocked about Lydia's death... but Marcia's? That could be a different story."

"And Julian seemed genuinely shattered by Marcia's death, also, correct?" Radleigh pointed out.

I nodded. Julian had *appeared* devastated; his polished exterior had cracked enough for me to glimpse raw emotion beneath, not to mention the blank space where the time-telling watch could have been.

Then again, Liz was just as shocked.

The rest of the sleepless evening was spent retracing steps, probing notes, and checking alibis and memories for missed details that might illuminate murky waters until we came up with a solid plan and were ready to press 'Go.'

I squinted at the glow of my phone screen, tapping out a message that would lure them into my web—a bit of tomfoolery, you might say, but desperate times called for desperate measures. I had to craft something so tantalizing and irresistible that Julian, Robert, Victor, and Liz would have no choice but to scuttle over to Lydia's shop like moths to a flame.

"Urgent: Lydia's and Marcia's secret's revealed tonight. Meet me at Lydia's shop. 8 PM sharp. -C. Critt."

I hit send on each text and watched the digital bait disappear into the ether. If any of them held the key to this kerfuffle, they'd bite the bait.

––––––

The day dragged on as I busied myself with preparations. Finally, at quarter to eight, I stationed myself behind Lydia's counter, Alfie taking up his stoic position beside me. Radleigh and Trixie took to their stations in the back room with a recording device and Charlie's number on speed dial should law enforcement be required.

The bell above the door jingled. Julian was the first to arrive, his rumpled suit traded for jeans and a sweater. "I must say, Carrigan, this is quite the fuss you're stirring up," he said.

"Julian," I nodded. "You came. You must've had a vested interest in all of this hoopla."

Before he could reply, the door chimed again—in strolled Robert Grant. His gaze darkened when it met Julian's, then flicked between us before settling on me. "Carrigan, what's this about Lydia and Marcia's secret?" he asked. His voice was calm, but his posture was rigid.

I smiled at him. "Oh, just some unfinished business they left behind. You'll see."

Victor strolled in next and paused questioningly when he saw the others in attendance, his eyes piercing the others as he took his place in the 'play.'

Liz was the last to enter, her expression unreadable beneath her perfectly styled hair. "So," she began cautiously, "we're all here for some big reveal, are we?"

The four stood before me in a quad of tension, each one bewildered by the others' presence and my vague invitation. They eyed one another with a mix of suspicion and intrigue.

The ghostly form of Lydia materialized beside me; only I could see her solemn visage as she glanced from suspect to suspect. Alfie rose and meowed loudly, walking across the counter to stare at Lydia's ghost. From the onlookers' perspective, it would have appeared that Alfie was staring into space, meowing at nothing.

Lydia's ethereal form tinged with the faintest lavender hue, just like her favorite scent. I could sense her anxiety, a silent storm of confusion brewing in her spectral eyes as she gazed at the gathered suspects. "Carrigan, what's happening?

Why are they here? Do they know who killed me?" She sucked in a sharp, ghostly breath. "Was it…one of them?"

I wanted to answer, to comfort her, to tell her I was on the cusp of unraveling the tangled web that led to her untimely demise. But I couldn't without giving my abilities away. I needed to tuck that bit of information in my back pocket— for now.

Lydia continued her voice, a desperate whisper that only I could hear. "I remember... there was an argument... someone came to the shop that night. Who was it?"

I ached to speak to her, to discuss this new revelation openly, but I couldn't risk it—not with this audience. So I nodded ever so slightly, hoping she'd understand that I was listening and believed her.

Lydia's face contorted in a silent plea for clarity. "They were angry about something—so angry—and then... nothing. It's all just bits and pieces."

Another imperceptible nod from me—barely a twitch, really—my acknowledgment locked behind a poker face. Lydia looked from me to them and back again, her expression morphing into one of realization as if a memory fragment had slotted into place.

But before that ethereal mouth could part with more ghostly revelations, the players in the room demanded my attention. With Lydia's whispers hanging in the air like mist over a graveyard, I turned back to the living—the suspects— my heart pounding against my ribs like a frantic drummer.

CHAPTER 19
DANGER & DISCOVERY

"YOU SEE," I addressed them all, feeling Lydia's spectral presence bolstering my resolve, "each of you had a motive tied up in secrets and lies—but only one went as far as murder."

I let the accusation hang, not expecting it to be claimed.

Julian's facade cracked just a sliver; he scoffed with a forced nonchalance that didn't quite mask his nerves. "And you think one of us must be involved because we responded to your cryptic message?"

I locked eyes with him. "Wouldn't *you* be curious if someone claimed to unearth your darkest secret?"

The room filled with an uneasy silence as they pondered their predicament—they were caught in a web of their own making simply by showing up.

"Look," Robert interjected with a sigh that suggested he was more nincompoop than a cold-blooded killer. "Lydia had many secrets. It doesn't mean we're murderers."

Liz nodded in agreement too quickly, her voice high-pitched and tinged with panic. "Exactly! I mean, what proof do you even have?"

Ah yes, proof—the bane of every snollygoster thinking they could outsmart me.

"Well," I started slowly, gauging their reactions as I spoke. Thankfully, Lydia was quite meticulous in her journaling—she had a knack for higgledy-piggledy details and all."

Julian crossed his arms. "And?"

"And," I continued, feeling Alfie rub against my arm for moral support, "she mentioned all of you often in her entries."

Robert cleared his throat uncomfortably while Liz's hand twitched and rose to her throat.

"Your initials were obvious. MW for Marcia Wells, JR for Julian, RG for Robert, and VV." I paused, eyeing Victor and Liz for any glimpse of surprise. They didn't disappoint. "Seems like both VVs wanted something valuable... something worth killing for." My words hung heavy like a Maine fog rolling off the bay.

I continued. "At first, I thought VV was Victor Venn until I learned that Liz's real name is Vivian. Vivian Vincent—VV."

Liz blinked rapidly, her hands twisting together nervously. Victor's jaw clenched, and he looked anywhere but at me.

"We know someone poisoned Lydia," I started slowly, allowing each word to settle before moving on to the next. Liz shifted uncomfortably at those words; Julian watched me closely as if trying to anticipate where I was going with this line of reasoning.

"The arsenic in her tea," Victor mused aloud.

"Yes. And we know that someone tried very hard to point fingers at Marcia for the crime," I continued, glancing at Liz, who avoided my eyes.

I sauntered over to Liz. She wore a barrette, its whimsical design almost enchanting—plastic with a few pearls—an exact match to the piece of broken barrette Alfie found in the floorboards of Lydia's shop. My fingers curled around the broken piece in my pocket.

"Nice barrette," I said.

Liz's smile faltered for a fraction of a second before she recovered. "Thanks. It's vintage."

I nodded, feigning admiration while my heart hammered against my ribs. "It's charming. I notice it's broken, however." I said, pulling out the broken shard and holding it up to her. "And matches perfectly with a broken piece we found in the shop after Lydia died."

The color drained from Liz's face. She reached up to her hair, smoothing it back and removing her barrette.

"I'll take that, please." I offered my hand. Through pursed lips, she obliged, setting the barrette in my palm. The barrette she wore was indeed the exact match to the pieces Alfie and I found.

Her eyes widened in alarm, but she didn't speak.

Alfie perched on the counter, his green eyes fixed on Liz, his tail flicking with an air of knowing that added weight to the silence in Lydia's shop. I took a deep breath, gathering my thoughts and the courage to lay out the puzzle pieces I'd meticulously fit together.

"Liz," I started, my voice steady despite the flutter in my chest, "I believe you came here the night Lydia died to meet with her, didn't you? To talk about your plans?"

Liz's face ashened. The room was thick with tension, a mix of anticipation and dread knotting in my stomach. "Yes," she confessed, her voice a whisper at first that grew stronger as she continued. "I hated Marcia. She took credit for everything I did—treated me like just one of her brushes or palettes: disposable. But I didn't kill her or Lydia."

"No, you played the long game with Lydia behind Marcia's back," I murmured more to myself than to Liz. "you befriended Lydia so you could conspire to create a line of cosmetics so grand that it would bury Marcia."

She nodded slowly. "I was going to meet Lydia here and have tea. We were going to talk about how to get back at Marcia. Lydia was sick of Marcia trying to steal her formulas, and I... I wanted more than just being someone's chemist and assistant."

"And when you arrived?" I prodded gently.

Liz swallowed hard, a single tear trailing down her cheek. "I found her d...dead." Her voice cracked as she clutched at the fabric of her dress. "She was already gone, Carrigan."

I leaned in closer, driven by empathy and the need for truth. "And the lipstick? The one from Marcia's vintage collection?"

She nodded, more tears now streaming freely down her face. "It was a spur-of-the-moment decision. I grabbed lipstick from the vintage display, applied a little lipstick to Lydia's lips, placed the tube near Lydia's hand, and...and I left. I hit my head on the counter when I got up. That must have been when I broke my barrette." She wiped her face angrily with the back of her hand. "I rearranged the lipstick tubes in the display case so the missing tube wasn't obvious to Marcia. I thought if Marcia took the fall for Lydia's death, it would clear my path to creating my own cosmetic line."

My heart raced as everything clicked into place—the missing lipstick from Marcia's exhibit, Lydia's lifeless body and stained lips, lying cold on the floor of this very shop.

My cell phone pinged. Alfie pawed at it and mewed loudly. I glanced at the name. Charlie. "Excuse me a moment." I opened the message;

Charlie: *"We found a match for the fingerprints we lifted from your home. They belong to one Rebecca Graves. She's an arsonist who's been on the run from the authorities for years."* Rebecca Graves, who in the thundering tarnation could that possibly be, and...

Three dots appeared. Charlie was texting more information.

"Reports say she blew up a rival cosmetic company just days before she started working for Marcia Wells."

I was gobsmacked and about to reply to Charlie when the three dots appeared again, showing more info was coming.

Except it wasn't more info; it was a picture.

Of Liz Vincent.

Charlie: *It would appear our Liz has a few secrets. I'm heading out to interview her now.*

Oh, fiddlesticks.

I couldn't let Charlie know I was having a rather heated tête-à-tête with Liz and *all* the remaining suspects in the two murders. I had to think–and act–fast. I wanted to text Charlie back but knew my clumsy fingers would not cooperate. I hit the little microphone button and held the phone to my lips.

Me: *"Gosh golly gumdrops, she has more secrets than Victoria herself! I am shocked at my very core. This is incredibly shocking news. I am just shocked. Good luck with the interview. I am busy doing normal evening things. Hair washing, tea bag organizing, cat bathing, and what have you. Okay, BYE!"*

Phew. That should throw him off the scent. High-five to me.

I turned back to the others, their expressions a mixture of confusion and curiosity. Suddenly, everything clicked into place. "So, you planted the lipstick tube to frame Marcia, Rebecca—"

Liz's straightened. "What? How did you—"

"Then, you broke into my house the other evening and completely ransacked the place, and to be honest, were quite sloppy about it–leaving fingerprints behind. What sort of devious pilferer are you? And what were you looking for?"

Liz stared at me in stunned disbelief.

"According to Deputy Best," I waved my phone at her, "you are wanted for arson. Something about starting a fire at another cosmetics company. Were they Marcia's rivals also? Were you planning to burn every other company down for your benefit?!" I was sweating now. Great. Soon, my calm, collected manner would show a prominent crack—sweat stains in my armpits.

"And when you learned of Marcia's death—from me, outside the Chatterbox Cafe—you already knew, and you had planted the bottle of arsenic in her bag to throw more suspicion on Marcia, just in case the lipstick tube wasn't enough." My voice was laced with disbelief at how far someone would go out of sheer ambition and spite.

"Yes," Liz murmured, defeat etched into every line of her face. "To all of it. But Marcia made me do it!" she cried, "she offered me an incredible salary if I agreed to set the fire and take down her rival! When I saw my opportunity to point Lydia's death in her direction, *I took it.* I planted the lipstick on Lydia. Marcia always insisted I arrive early to set up the festival booth. When I got there, I discovered her body. I was terrified, but it gave me another opportunity to point Lydia's death in her direction. I tossed the contents of her bag next to her and planted the bottle of arsenic there. I broke into your house to find Lydia's formulas."

"You knew I had them?"

"Yes. After the police were done with their investigation, I went to her shop to break in and find them. I saw you and your friends go in and then leave. I saw you tuck them into your bag. So I broke into your place when you were gone for the evening to find them."

Liz's shoulders slumped as if relieved by unburdening herself of this secret she'd carried since that fateful night.

Lydia's ghost wavered beside me. "She's telling the truth, Carrigan! Liz didn't kill me! I remember now!" Lydia exclaimed, her hands clasped together as if in prayer.

I glanced at her ghost, giving her a subtle nod to acknowledge her input without drawing attention from the living. "Okay, thank you. I'm glad we got that bit settled," I murmured.

Liz's gaze snapped to mine, mistaking my response as

directed at her. "You believe me?" she asked, hope lacing her voice.

"Yes," I replied in a measured tone. "I believe you didn't kill Lydia. Although you must answer for your deception, arson, and ransacking of my house…shall I make a list? I better make a list." I reached for a piece of paper.

Liz let out a shaky breath, relief visibly sagging her shoulders. "No, that's fine. Thank you," she whispered.

With that small scene closed, I turned to the rest of the group.

Julian still looked skeptical; his arms crossed over his chest as if he were bracing against a storm. Robert appeared more bewildered than anything else—clearly out of his depth in this twisty tale of cosmetics and vengeance. Victor was silent but watchful, his eyes sharp as flint.

"Now," I began again, feeling Lydia's supportive presence beside me, "we've established that Liz didn't kill Lydia. That means we're back to square one with three potential suspects." I let that sink in for a moment before continuing. "But let's not forget the second murder—Marcia's death is just as important in this twisted narrative."

Julian shifted uncomfortably. "Sounds like 'Liz' here had the most motive…"

I sighed heavily; it was time to push harder if we were going to unravel this mystery once and for all.

"Let's talk about motives for *both* murders," I suggested firmly. "Starting with you, Julian."

CHAPTER 20

LOVE & BETRAYAL

THE TENSION in the room stretched thin like cobwebs in an attic window—fragile yet clinging stubbornly to old wood.

Julian Ravenscroft, with an attitude you only get from a lifetime of silver spoons and private schools, looked every bit the untouchable elite as he stood across from me in Lydia's shop. But untouchable didn't mean uninvolved, and as much as I wanted to find a cozy corner to crochet my worries away, it was time to pull at some threads.

"So Julian," I began, letting Alfie curl up on a patch of early moonlight on the counter, "you've got quite the vested interest in Marcia's well-being—or rather, you had."

His smile was practiced, the kind that never reached his eyes. "Marcia was more than just a client to me, Carrigan. Her death is... it's devastating."

I nodded. "You're a man of influence, power. And let's not mince words—you had the motive."

"Motive?" His laugh was hollow.

I tilted my head slightly, keeping my gaze locked on his. "Love? Betrayal? You knew about Marcia and Robert Grant's little dalliance."

Julian's facade cracked just enough for a flicker of anger to pass through his eyes before he smoothed it over with another one of those smiles."That doesn't make me a killer."

"No," I agreed, "but it does make you human. Humans do foolish things when their hearts get tangled up in knots."

"Look," he said with a sigh that sounded more like resignation than defeat, "I won't pretend I wasn't angry with Marcia. Hurt even. But murder? That's not me."

I nodded slowly but didn't break eye contact. "Maybe not," I said softly. "But you and Marcia both had motive to see Lydia's demise..."

Julian straightened his sweater. "You have quite the imagination, Miss Critt," he said coldly.

"Lydia mentioned you both in her journals. You were 'up to no good,' as she put it. What were you and Marcia after, Julian?"

Julian shifted uncomfortably. "Lydia was using our formulas for her products."

"Our?" I arched an eyebrow.

He hesitated but then straightened his back as if deciding. "Yes, ours. Marcia and I wanted them back."

Victor snorted. "The formulas belonged to my family all along. Marcia's family stole them from me!"

Julian turned to him with a scowl. "You have no proof of that, Victor."

I held up a hand before Victor could retort. "Let's cut through the hullabaloo, shall we? Lydia had the formulas, Julian—and she was planning on selling them back to Victor."

"Extortion? My Lydia?" Robert gasped.

"Let me lay it out for you," I said calmly but firmly. "Marcia's family stole from the Venns—bankrupted them—then Lydia pilfered the Venn Family formulas from Marcia."

The room erupted into a cacophony of arguing.

I steadied my breath as Lydia's specter shimmered into view, the edges of her form blurring like watercolors caught in the rain. The others, oblivious to her ghostly presence, continued their heated exchange, but I could only focus on her. Lydia looked different this time—clearer as if the fog that clouded her memory had lifted.

She hovered close, and her voice, a soft murmur only I could hear, broke through the clamor. "Carrigan, I remember now."

I nodded subtly to acknowledge her, keeping my eyes on the living. "You were trying to extort from Victor, weren't you?" I whispered.

"Yes," Lydia whispered, and I felt a chill despite the room's warmth. "I can't believe I did that. I was going to sell him back his family's formulas."

"Why?" I asked softly, not expecting her to have an answer.

"I wanted to secure my future." Lydia's voice trembled with a cocktail of shame and resolve. "I knew Marcia was ruthless—she'd do anything to keep her edge in the business, and I was right. She and Julian started a court case against me, claiming I had stolen 'their' formulas. I had to protect myself and build my empire with Liz's help. I needed the money from Victor to do so."

"Lydia," I pressed gently, "did you intend to go through with it? Extort money from Victor, I mean?"

Her gaze met mine—a torrent of regret in her eyes. "I—I don't know. At first, it seemed like justice for Victor's family... then it just became about survival in the industry."

A silence hung heavy in the room as Lydia's confession echoed in my mind alone. Alfie jumped down from the counter and brushed against my leg.

"SURVIVAL!" I yelled to the group to gain their attention. They all heard me and stopped their bickering. "Lydia was afraid of losing everything she'd built," I said—to Lydia and everyone else in the room.

Robert ran a hand through his hair in frustration. "And now she's lost even more."

Victor crossed his arms over his chest, his face etched with lines of bitter understanding. "It seems we've all been playing a dangerous game."

"And who stands to gain from this the most?" Julian asked with an intensity that bordered on desperation.

"That's what we're here to figure out." My gaze flickered briefly to Lydia's spirit before returning to Julian, Victor, and Robert—a trio burdened by their secrets and desires. Each one had something to lose or gain from this tangled web we found ourselves in. But who among them would kill for it?

"Julian, you and Marcia were taking Lydia to court to regain the formulas. Walk us through that, please." I asked.

Julian gave me a look of surprise. "How did you know? It's true. We…Marcia and I were taking Lydia to court over the formulas."

"Julian, was there proof that Lydia had stolen Victor's formulas from Marcia? Proof that would stand up in court?" I asked.

Julian nodded his head. "Yes, we had video footage of someone–we believed it to be Lydia–taking the notecards from a locked compartment in Marcia's desk."

"You said 'someone'. So, you weren't sure it was Lydia?"

Julian bowed his head. "No, not absolute. But, close enough that I believed we had a solid case and was prepared to argue that in court."

"I see," I looked from Julian to Liz. "It was you, wasn't it?"

Julian looked momentarily confused. "What? She? Oh!"

Liz's face turned an impressive shade of rouge. "Yes, it was me," she whispered, her voice barely audible. "But I didn't know those were the Venn family formulas. I thought they were Marcia's family formulas."

"But why steal them from Marcia? What did you have to gain?"

"Because…Lydia asked me to. We were working together

to bring Marcia's empire down. If we had her family formulas, we'd have leverage. There are a lot of ingredients in those old formulas that are no longer approved—"

"And you planned to include some of those ingredients in Marcia's current formulations?" I asked, the puzzle pieces clicking together.

Liz nodded. "All it would take was one batch and an anonymous call to the FDA inspectors. If I–we–had the formulas in our possession, we could say that Marcia was forcing me to create products that didn't adhere to modern standards."

"You conniving little witch," Julian stepped toward Liz, then stopped and turned to me. "You're sure she didn't kill Marcia? Sounds like she's got tons of motive."

"Oh, I'm sure, Julian. Yes, she had a motive but didn't have the most to gain. Robert," I said, turning towards Lydia's estranged husband, "you had the most to gain from Lydia's death. With her gone, everything she built would be yours."

He held my stare, his eyes glassy. "You think I killed Lydia for the estate?" His voice was laced with an edge that hadn't been there before. "I didn't care about the damn shop or the business. It was a divorce I wanted. I wanted to be with Marcia. Lydia wanted to work on our marriage. I wanted out."

"You wanted Marcia?" Julian's voice cut through the silence like a knife.

Robert's gaze shifted to Julian. "Yes, of course," Robert confirmed, a rawness creeping into his tone. "Marcia was... she was everything Lydia wasn't. Ambitious, fierce—"

"—Manipulative," Liz interjected bitterly.

He shot her a look but continued. "Yes, she had her ways. But she was alive in a way Lydia never was."

Victor leaned forward, his curiosity piqued. "And you think that's enough to clear your name? Love as an alibi?"

"I don't need an alibi," Robert snapped back. "I didn't kill Lydia."

Julian paced. "But Lydia wouldn't give you a divorce so you could be with another woman–*my woman*? That screams motive to me!" his voice was rising to a fever pitch.

Lydia's ghost hovered near me, her expression sorrowful yet searching—urging me to find the truth buried beneath layers of deception.

"Is that true?" I whispered to her.

Lydia's ghost looked down and nodded. "I knew he was having an affair, but I loved him. I wanted to work on our marriage. I begged him to stay in our home, to work on things, and I thought we were…" a single ghostly tear ran down her cheek.

I sighed and crossed my arms, considering Robert's words.

"No, you didn't kill Lydia, Robert." I said quietly, "But you did kill Marcia."

CHAPTER 21

TENSION & TRUTHS

GASPS ECHOED THROUGH THE SHOP.

Robert met my gaze squarely, and I saw something break open in his eyes—a fissure revealing a depth of emotion he'd kept hidden. "No! I loved her," he said quietly, "I couldn't…"

Liz snorted in disbelief, but I held up my hand to silence her before she could speak.

Victor scoffed. "Love is as much a motive as money."

"Except," I interjected before Victor could continue down that path, "Robert didn't need to kill Lydia for money or love. If what he says is true—that it was Marcia he wanted—then Lydia's death wouldn't have given him what he desired. He could have left Lydia anytime, but for some reason, he stayed."

"I wanted to leave, I did. But Marcia…she kept stalling. Saying we'd be together soon…" Robert answered. "I had little choice but to stay in our home until Marcia said otherwise…"

Julian frowned at that logic. "But he *must* have done it. With Lydia out of the way, he'd have her money *and* Marcia… not that she'd have you!" Julian, eyes wild, pointed at Robert.

"Robert didn't kill Lydia," I said again, firmly.

Victor turned towards me; his expression hardened by skepticism. "If Robert didn't kill Lydia–which seems the most obvious conclusion–then who? You've brought us here for answers, dammit."

"Yes," Julian echoed impatiently. "Let's have them, Carrigan."

I took a deep breath and looked at each of them—Robert with his shattered dreams; Julian with his bruised ego; Victor with his smoldering vendetta; and Liz with her chameleon facade—all players in this deadly game where Lydia and Marcia had become unwilling pawns.

"Robert," I began, "you know you were just a pawn in Marcia's game, don't you? A means to an end to get to Lydia's coveted botanical formulas."

He shifted uncomfortably." I don't know what you're talking about," he muttered. "Marcia said she loved me and wanted to be with me." But his eyes betrayed him, filled with fear and anger.

I leaned forward. "Oh, but I think you do. Marcia was playing you. She never loved you—it was Julian she loved. They were together in this scheme—taking Lydia to court over formulas that weren't even Marcia's to claim. But she kept her relationship with Julian a secret from you. You met with Marcia in Portland the night of Lydia's death, didn't you?"

The words hung heavy between us, and I could see the realization dawning on him. His face turned a shade paler as he absorbed the blow. He shook his head in denial. "Yes. She told me it would be our last secret meeting. She said she loved me and wanted to be with me. *Me!*"

I reached out and gently touched his arm. "Robert, she was using you. It was never about love; it was about profit and revenge."

He recoiled from my touch as if burned by the raw truth. His eyes were now wild with emotions he could no longer contain.

"You were there that morning at the festival grounds," I pressed on, watching as each word struck him like the physical blow he made to Marcia. "After everything came crashing down when you found out that she was with Julian—the lies, the deceit—you confronted her." I reached into my pocket and pulled out my phone, opening the photo of the broken watch. "Robert, look at this," I said, extending the phone towards him.

He hesitated momentarily before taking it, his fingers brushing against mine. The tension in the room felt like a physical force as he stared at the photo, his face unreadable.

"Do you recognize this watch?" I asked, watching his reaction closely.

Robert's eyes flickered to meet mine, then returned to the phone. He said nothing, but I saw the slightest twitch at the corner of his mouth, the briefest narrowing of his eyes. "It looks familiar," he finally said, handing back my phone with care that seemed exaggerated.

I nodded slowly. "Mind if I see your wrist?"

He seemed to consider resisting for a second, then sighed and pushed up his sleeve. The pale strip of skin where a watch would usually sit was stark against his tanned forearm —a perfect match for the size and shape of the watch in the photo.

"Looks like you wear one about this size," I observed casually, but my heart pounded. It was another piece of this convoluted puzzle slotting into place.

Robert pulled his sleeve back down hastily. "Lots of people wear watches," he muttered defensively. "It could have just as easily been Julian."

"That's what I thought, also, but then..." I nodded toward

Julian, "Show me your watch, please, Julian?" Julian pulled back his sleeve. On his wrist was a watch with a larger face that glinted under the shop's lights. The tan lines on his arm told their own story—a watch regularly worn matched the tan lines underneath.

"See? It's much larger than Robert's style here." My eyes darted between the two men, taking in every detail. "My point is that whoever hit Marcia left this bit of evidence behind at the scene of the crime."

The room seemed to shrink around us as implications hung like cobwebs—tenuous and sticky. Robert shifted uncomfortably beside me; even Alfie picked up on the unease and retreated to a corner.

Robert glanced nervously at Julian before turning back to me. "Carrigan, this is ridiculous," he protested weakly. "You can't seriously think—"

I cut him off sharply. "Yes, Robert, that is exactly what I'm thinking."

The accusation hung there between us. Julian stepped closer now, his chest puffed—but I stood my ground and stepped between the two men.

"You two have been dancing around each other since before Marcia died when you discovered the truth about each other on the festival grounds. We witnessed your argument." I nodded toward Victor, then continued steadily. "But it's time for the music to stop." My gaze flicked from Robert's tense face to Julian's carefully composed one.

Robert's hands clenched into fists, his knuckles white with tension. "I loved her," he growled through gritted teeth.

"And yet," I continued, my voice soft but unyielding, "when you realized Marcia's affections were all part of her scheme—when you saw her with Julian—it broke something inside you."

He looked away then, lost somewhere in the past that

played out like scenes from a tragic play—one where he had been cast as the fool.

"You killed her," I said quietly but firmly. "In a passionate rage when you realized she'd never loved you—she was just using you to get to Lydia's formulas."

Alfie let out a low mewl from his perch—a sound that seemed to resonate with the sorrow and betrayal that filled the room.

Robert buried his face in his hands before looking up at me again. His eyes shimmered with unshed tears. "I didn't mean to," he whispered hoarsely. "It just... happened. I went to the festival grounds early to talk to her. To make her realize she loved me, not...*him...*," he pointed at Julian. "But when I saw her there, setting up, I pictured them together and I just...snapped. I couldn't believe she'd lied to me all this time..."

The confession hung there—raw and jagged.

"Robert, where's the murder weapon?" I asked.

Robert fiddled with his sleeve, covering the blank space where the tell-a-tale watch had been. "A hammer I found near one of the vendor tables. I...tossed it in the ocean."

Julian's eyes flickered with the intensity of a coming storm, his breath hot and fast through flared nostrils. He spat out, "You bastard! You killed her! She was everything to me!"

A scoff escaped Robert. "You were a means to an end, just like me. Once she'd got the formulas from Lydia, you would have been yesterday's news."

The air crackled as Julian stepped closer to Robert, their faces inches apart. I could feel the tension, a tangible force that seemed to press against my chest. Alfie, sensing the energy shift, let out a low growl.

"You know nothing about our relationship," Julian hissed.

"Enough!" Liz's voice pierced the standoff. "This isn't helping anything."

Victor stood back, arms crossed over his chest, watching the scene unfold with a calculating gaze.

Lydia's ghost lingered by my side, her expression one of sorrow and regret. In an instant, the room exploded into chaos as Julian lunged at Robert with a fury that seemed to come from the depths of his soul. Robert reacted instinctively, throwing up his hands to defend himself as they grappled with each other.

"Stop it!" I shouted over their grunts and curses. Alfie darted away from the fray, hiding behind a display case.

As they fought, knocking over displays and sending products flying across the room, Julian's demeanor shifted. His punches became more desperate—less about defense and more about unleashing something pent up inside him.

"You took her from me!" Julian roared at Robert between blows.

Robert pushed Julian back against a counter, his anger fueled by accusation and grief.

"Enough!" My voice finally broke through their rage as I wedged myself between them once more, pushing them apart with all my strength.

They stumbled away from each other, chests heaving and faces marked with scratches and bruises.

Lydia's ghost watched them with an expression that mirrored my heartache—a mix of pity and frustration at the destructive power of secrets kept too long in the dark.

Julian wiped the blood from his lip with the back of his hand. His eyes were wild, but beneath that, there was pain— raw and unfiltered.

"It was never supposed to go this far," Robert muttered. "I loved her... I loved Marcia."

The room fell silent again—every eye on Robert as he stood there exposed in his confession.

"We know you loved her," I said softly. "But love can make people do crazy things."

He laughed bitterly at that—a sound devoid of any genuine humor. "You have no idea."

But I did have an idea. The puzzle pieces had fallen into place, each slotting in with a satisfying click in my mind. Alfie jumped up on the counter again, his green eyes unblinking, watching the drama unfold with feline indifference.

I turned to the last remaining suspect. "Well, Victor, it all comes down to you."

CHAPTER 22

THREATS & THROATS

VICTOR VENN STOOD BEFORE ME, his face a mask of calm.

"Victor," I began, my voice steady despite the drumming of my heart. "You came to Lydia's shop that night with a promise, didn't you? You told her you had the money she was asking for—the price to get back what belonged to your family."

Victor's composure faltered for a moment, but he recovered quickly. "Lydia and I were negotiating. There was no need for what you're implying."

I locked eyes with him, letting my gaze bore into his. "But there *was* a need, wasn't there? Lydia had something you wanted desperately—the formulas that could restore your family's legacy."

A flicker of something dark crossed Victor's face before he masked it with a practiced smile. "You're reaching at straws, Carrigan. These other goons had just as much–if not more–motive than me."

Alfie let out a soft meow as if to challenge Victor's denial. I ignored him and pressed on.

My words sliced through the tension in the room. "Your

alibi for Lydia's murder was tickets to a conference, but the attendance records for each meeting show that you never arrived—a perfect alibi if you actually attended them."

Victor straightened up, his hands clenched at his sides now. "And what would that prove? That I'm not proactive about networking? I was there. They must have marked it wrong."

I shook my head slowly. "No, Victor. It proves that you were trying to create an alibi where there wasn't one." I let those words hang in the air before delivering the final blow. "I checked with the organizers and speakers. They confirmed your absence despite your name being on their lists."

The color drained from Victor's face as realization dawned on him—the game was up.

"I have to admit, I wasn't completely convinced that you killed Lydia," I faced him directly, my voice rising in anger and certainty. "Until this evening, when you mentioned the arsenic in Lydia's tea. You couldn't have known that unless you were part of the official murder investigation or..." I jabbed a finger into his chest, "*You* poisoned her tea with arsenic because she was blackmailing you over those formulas. When Deputy Best and I were in the back room, you returned to the shop to hunt for the formulas. *These* formulas." I pulled the Venn Family formula notecards from my bag. A soft gasp from the onlookers filled the room.

Victor's jaw clenched, his eyes darting around as if seeking an escape route. The shop felt smaller suddenly, closing in on us as the gravity of the accusation pulled us all toward its center.

"Carrigan," he started, but I cut him off.

"No more lies, Victor! No more hiding behind fake alibis or pretending to be a harmless genealogist!" My hand shook slightly as I pointed the notecards at him, fueled by a desire for justice for Lydia's death.

The room had become a pressure cooker, and Victor Venn

was the valve ready to burst. I felt every pair of eyes on me, some wide with fear, others narrowed with suspicion. I took a deep breath, trying to steady the thundering pulse in my ears. Alfie, always my barometer for the strange and uncanny, let out a warning growl from his perch on the counter.

Lydia's ghost flickered into view like a bad television signal before steadying into a translucent figure. Her presence sent a chill down my spine, not out of fear but from the sudden drop in temperature her appearance always brought. She looked more solid than before; her form sharpened with purpose and memory.

"Lydia," I whispered, keeping my eyes fixed on Victor's increasingly desperate face.

He couldn't see her; none of them could. But Lydia had been my unseen ace from the start—my spectral informant whose fragmented memories were the missing pieces to this puzzle.

She floated closer to me, and though I knew she couldn't physically touch me, I felt the weight of her gaze like a hand on my shoulder. "Carrigan," Lydia said, her voice echoing in my head rather than filling the room. "I remember now. You're right. It was Victor." Her words were soft but laced with steel. "He came to my shop that evening under the guise of peace," Lydia continued. "He said he was excited to get his family formulas back and held no grudge against me. He made me tea..." Her voice trailed off, the recollection of her murder too much to bear. "He said it was a new blend he wanted me to celebrate." Lydia's spectral form shuddered as though reliving the betrayal afresh. "I trusted him. I drank it without question."

As I relayed Lydia's account to those gathered, the room remained silent as a grave.

"Victor Venn brought tea for Lydia that night," I announced firmly. "A special blend he to celebrate getting his family formulas back. He told Lydia he didn't hold a grudge against her for harboring the formulas–and for her extortion."

Victor's adamancy cracked like thin ice underfoot; his eyes flickered to where Lydia hovered—a look of guilt betraying him despite not seeing her. "How…how could you know…?" he began but faltered under the collective scrutiny of the room.

Lydia moved closer to him, and though he was oblivious to her spectral proximity, his body reacted with an involuntary shiver. "He was definitely here," she said firmly, each word etched in certainty. "He made the tea. I drank it and blacked out." Her revelation hung like a dark cloud about to burst.

I turned to Victor again, my resolve hardened by Lydia's confirmation. "Lydia remembers your visit and that special tea you were so eager for her to taste."

Victor's face paled further; his lips moved soundlessly as he searched for an alibi that wouldn't come. "Lydia…? But she's…"

"Dead, yes. Didn't I mention it? I can see, hear, and speak to ghosts."

Lydia's ghost rewarded me with a smile.

The room erupted into murmurs and movement as Victor's composure finally shattered under the weight of accusation and evidence. His gaze darted around frantically; his previous suave demeanor was replaced by panic and fear. It was like watching an animal caught in a trap—it would fight viciously but ultimately knew escape was impossible.

I locked eyes with him one last time before he lunged.

———

Victor grabbed me by the neck and moved behind me, pulling me into him with one arm. With the other, he grabbed a letter opener off the counter and held it to my side.

"Ow! Watch it!" I gasped, my throat constricting. I pulled at his hand with my free one, but he tightened his grip.

Julian made a move toward us.

"Stop right there. Everyone back up!" Victor yelled, jabbing the letter-opener into my side, poking me hard. Julian put his hands up and backed off.

The shop brimmed with tension, like a pot on the verge of boiling over. Lydia's ghost hovered in the corner, her translucent figure flickering with the dim light that filtered through the dusty windows. Victor, my neck still firmly in his grasp, barked, "Grab the formulas." I snatched them off the counter. Julian, Robert, and Liz were scattered around the room, eyes wide.

Ever the enigmatic feline, Alfie prowled the edges of the scene, his tail swishing with a hunter's precision.

Victor's eyes darted toward the door, a clear intent to skedaddle written all over his face.

"Now, hold on just a tick," Julian said, stepping into his path. "You're not going anywhere."

He scoffed and made a break for it, dragging me with him. But before we could reach the door, Alfie leaped from his shadowy vigil with the agility of an acrobat. In one swift motion, Alfie latched onto Victor's head with claws unsheathed.

"Alfie!" I gasped as Victor stumbled, releasing me, his escape thwarted by ten pounds of determined tabby.

Victor screamed at Alfie while trying to shake him off. "Get this mangy beast off me!" Alfie dug in harder. Blood tracked down Victor's temples, neck, and face.

I stepped forward, shoving Victor against the wall where he crumpled as Alfie launched off of Victor's head and into my arms. "Good job, Alfie!" I coughed, giving him a quick squeeze before letting him go.

Alfie sauntered back toward Victor, positioning himself between Victor's feet with a look of triumph in his green eyes.

Victor huffed in frustration and moaned in pain, holding his head, blood oozing from between his fingers.

Meanwhile, Robert had edged closer to the direction of Lydia's office and back exit—a desperate look on his face signaling his intent to bolt. He glanced between Julian and me as if weighing his odds.

Before he could move, I lunged across the room just as Trixie and Radleigh came out from their hiding place, much to Robert's shock. Radleigh snagged him by the collar of his shirt.

"And just where do you think you're going?"

Robert spun around, surprise etched into every line on his face. "Carrigan! What—"

"No more running," I said firmly.

The rest of the room stood frozen. Liz's eyes were wide with shock; Julian had raised an eyebrow in interest; even Lydia's spirit seemed more animated than usual.

"Both of you have some explaining to do to the police," I stated pointedly. "Don't start thinking you could just hightail it outta here without facing the music."

Both men slumped in defeat.

Lydia floated closer now; her spectral presence seemed to soak up every detail of this kerfuffle like she was piecing together her fragmented memories.

Liz broke the silence with a nervous chuckle. "Seems like Carrigan's got everything under control."

A smirk played on my lips despite the situation at hand. "You better believe it," I said confidently. "Radleigh? Trixie? You can call Charlie now."

"We already did, honey, and got everything on tape," Radleigh announced with a flourish, holding Robert by the shirt with one hand and a recorder in the other, high above his head like a shiny new trophy.

"Charlie's on his way," Trixie said, barely containing her excitement.

Victor and Robert looked at each other in resignation; their fates were sealed. Sirens wailed in the background, and Alfie howled in response.

A moment later, Charlie and his deputies burst in, his amber eyes taking in the scene with an efficiency that never ceased to amaze me. "Looks like you've had quite the party here," he said dryly as he stepped over the threshold.

I shrugged. "Just another day at the office," I quipped back, trying to sound nonchalant despite my racing heart.

Charlie's eyes flashed in anger. "Miss Critt. I figured something was off when you told me you were organizing your tea bags, but I never imagined this–questioning a room full of murder suspects?"

"Charlie, I–"

Charlie held up a hand, silencing me, as his gaze fell on Liz. "Rebecca Graves, I was just looking for you. Lovely to arrest you." He tipped his hat at Liz as one of his deputies cuffed her. "Victor Venn and Robert Grant. I trust there's a good reason you two look like you've been caught stealing from the cookie jar."

"Better than good," I replied. "They're involved in Lydia's murder. And Marcia's, too." I filled him in on everything as his officers cuffed the men and hauled all three of them out to the awaiting cars, reading them their rights as they went.

Charlie listened intently. Once I finished recounting the events leading up to this momentous occasion in Lydia's shop, I handed him the recording device. "We recorded their confessions," I announced proudly. "And here are the formulas that they have all been after." I handed the stack of notecards and Lydia's notebook over to Charlie.

Charlie nodded sharply. "I see," he said, "Miss Critt, this is excellent work, but let me get something straight. You've had these in your possession the entire time?"

I nodded, the hairs on my neck prickling. "Erm, yes. Yes."

"So, you withheld evidence from the police?"

Bumfuzzle.

"And, you gathered and questioned not just one but two murderers?"

Drat.

"Carrigan, attempting to question murderers is a risky game. You could have been hurt." Charlie's tone softened. "You must learn to trust me if we're going to work together in the future."

I stared at him in stunned disbelief, ignoring that he used my first name or mentioned having any kind of 'future' with me. "Charlie, I had offered–on several occasions–to help with the investigation, but you refused. You, sir, need to learn to trust *me!* I have certain abilities that—"

"Your ghost-whispering abilities, you mean? They didn't appear to be all that useful last time you tried them." He was referring to our prior meeting in this very shop.

Thrusting my hands firmly on my hips, I retorted, "Deputy Best, I most certainly have an 'other-worldly' edge for investigating a murder. Ask anybody. Ask Lydia's ghost. Lydia, show him!" I nodded toward Lydia, hovering near the scene. She picked up on the cue, took a deep breath, and swiped at a shelf full of products. Several bottles and jars flew from the shelf and scattered onto the floor.

Charlie's eyes widened. "What the…?"

"See, Charlie? This ability makes me a worthy ally of the police force, wouldn't you agree?"

Charlie rewarded me with a shake of his adorable head and a delightful, lopsided grin. "Let's hope we never have to test that theory." His voice was calm but carried an authoritative weight that echoed off the walls. "I'd like to question you further, Carrigan, perhaps at—"

"Listen, Charlie," I say, cutting him off. "As much as I would love to discuss things further over a glass of wine before the fire, we should get these delinquents back to the station. Even though all of this crime-solving has me craving alcohol and a foot rub, I don't think giving into our animalistic urges would be appropriate right now."

"Carrigan, I was only going to suggest that we continue the questioning at the station. Sorry to disappoint…"

Well, heck.

I can feel the redness creeping up my neck as I try to figure out how to dislodge my enormous foot from my larger mouth.

"Right, no, absolutely. That's what I was saying. Totally agree, you're right. That's why you're the best of the best, sir!"

Charlie stifled a grin. "Great. I'm glad that's settled. Julian Ravenscroft, you'll ride with me back to the station. I have a few questions for you, too." Charlie turned toward me, gave me a small salute, and walked out.

I smiled with a twinge of sadness at how things had turned out. Lives had been lost, secrets unearthed, and the town would buzz with gossip…

And I had funerals to plan.

CHAPTER 23
ENDINGS & ETHERS

WHEN EVERYONE, including Radleigh and Trixie, trickled out of Lydia's shop, their voices and footsteps fading into the brisk Castle Point air, I locked the door behind them, a hollow click echoing in the empty space. My ever-present feline shadow, Alfie, wound around my ankles, purring a soft rumble in the silence.

I turned to face Lydia's ghost, hovering near where she'd taken her last breath. The shop felt colder than it should have, not just from the Maine chill seeping through the windows. Lydia's spectral form glowed with dim light, her expression a mix of clarity and regret.

"Thanks for making a scene, then." I nodded toward the now-empty shelf and pile of bottles and jars on the floor.

Lydia smiled. "That was fun."

"You remember everything now, don't you?" I asked gently.

Lydia nodded. "I do, Carrigan. And I'm ashamed." Her voice quivered like autumn leaves on the cusp of winter.

Alfie leaped onto a display counter and sat regally, watching us with wide eyes.

"Lydia," I said softly, stepping closer to her wavering

figure. "We all get catawampus sometimes, veering off our intended paths."

She chuckled weakly at my choice of words. "Only you would use 'catawumpus' to describe my predicament."

I shrugged. "Sometimes we need whimsy to deal with the ballyhoo of life... or death."

Lydia's lips curved. "You have such an odd way of comforting people."

"It's one of my many charms," I joked lightly before growing serious again. "But listen, Lydia, holding onto regret won't help you find peace."

"I know." She sighed, the sound of a whispering wind through leaves long gone.

Alfie meowed softly as if offering his own brand of solace.

Lydia glanced around her shop—a spectral proprietress taking stock one last time. "It was my life's work, yet it led me here."

"It led you astray," I corrected gently. "But that doesn't diminish what you've accomplished or who you truly are."

She seemed flabbergasted by the idea—the possibility that she could still be seen as more than her ultimate mistake. "Carrigan," she started hesitantly, "do you think I'll be stuck in my shop forever?"

My heart swelled with compassion for this lost soul standing before me. "You can still make things right."

"How?" The single word hung between us like a lifeline dangling over an abyss.

"You let go," I told her simply. "You let go of the guilt and embrace forgiveness—forgiveness for yourself most of all."

A ghostly tear glistened in Lydia's eye as she considered my words. "And then?"

"And then you cross over," I breathed. "You move on to join the great being of light in the sky."

Her eyes flickered, grappling with ethereal concepts—and

then closed. Alfie purred louder now; even he seemed to sense the shift in energy as Lydia let go of her earthly ties.

The air grew warmer somehow, charged with lightness as Lydia took a step forward—or perhaps upward would be more accurate. Her form brightened, illuminating patches of floorboards and shelves laden with creams and powders that promised beauty but could never grant peace—not like this moment could.

"Thank you," she whispered gratefully.

"You're welcome," I replied with a half-smile and a sense of purpose that filled every corner of my being.

Lydia took another step and faded—a gentle dissipation into whatever lay beyond this world—and with each fading wisp of her presence, a weight lifted from both our shoulders: hers from guilt and mine from the burden of helping another lost spirit find their way home.

Alfie let out a soft mewl—a goodbye or maybe an acknowledgment that our job here was done—as Lydia's ghost disappeared completely, leaving behind only memories and a lesson learned in both life and death: forgiveness is not just a gift we give others; it is also one we must bestow upon ourselves.

I stood there for several long moments after she'd gone— the silence not so hollow anymore but filled with quiet triumph—and finally turned off the lights and locked Lydia's shop one last time before heading home with Alfie trotting loyally by my side.

––––––––

Alfie's purring rumbled like a tiny motor against my chest, his whiskers tickling my nose as the first slivers of dawn crept through the curtains. "Mornin', Alf," I mumbled, feeling the weight of his furry body pinning me to the bed. I stretched beneath him, and he protested with a gruff meow before resettling with a huff.

I patted his head, my mind churning with the day's tasks. It was closing day at the festival, and I had the somber duty of shipping Marcia's body to her family in Portland, attending the station to give Charlie all of my notes and sworn statement, and making Lydia's funeral arrangements. I sighed. Even thinking about it knotted my stomach.

Rolling out of bed, I dislodged Alfie, who protested with a dramatic flick of his tail before racing to the kitchen for his kibble. I scooped coffee into the maker in the kitchen and set it to brew. The rich aroma soon filled the air, promising a semblance of normalcy on a day that was anything but.

I grabbed the unopened stack of mail and my notepad from the counter. Cup in hand, I stepped onto my back deck, letting the cool morning air wash over me.

The sun peeked over the horizon, casting a warm glow across Castle Point. The quaint town was waking up; birds chirped cheerfully in the trees, and I knew the vendors would be preparing for their last day at the festival grounds.

Sitting down on a weathered chair, I sipped my coffee slowly. The steam curled up into the crisp air as I sorted through a stack of mail, reminding me of the note my father left me in Mr. Thompson's effects. I sighed. "What the devil happened to you, Dad?" I whispered to the birds, who chirped in answer. Besides the obvious–hit-and-run–I couldn't shake the feeling something else was afoot.

Another mystery for another day…

Taking a deep breath, I flipped open my notepad, ready to make a very long list of tasks for the day. I took another sip of hot go-go juice and stared out at my garden, now put to bed for the winter, letting its tranquility seep into me. There was much to do today, but this moment of quiet reflection was mine alone.

A chirpy "Good morning, Carrigan!" jolted me from my

serene bubble. I looked up, nearly choking on my coffee, as Horace's grinning face appeared over the fence, his eyes scanning down to my flannel-clad form.

"Horace! Privacy!" I sputtered, coffee splashing over my hand and onto the notepad—blurring ink across the paper.

He chuckled, a mischievous twinkle in his eye. "Now, now, don't be like that. I just wanted to greet my favorite neighbor!"

I rolled my eyes so hard I feared they might get stuck that way. "Keep your hello's to yourself next time—or at least wait until after I've had my second cup." Horace had a habit of pushing the boundaries of neighborly etiquette. He meant no harm, but his timing could've been better. Like maybe never. "And keep your nose on your side of the fence," I added with mock sternness.

He leaned on his elbows, propping himself up like a nosy squirrel. "You look all cozy in your jammies there."

I glanced down at myself and shrugged. At least I was decent—in flannel pajamas today, covered in cartoon ghosts —a nod to my otherworldly friends. It was not exactly in high fashion, but it was comfortable and ironically appropriate.

"Flannel is a girl's best friend with a neighbor like you." I quipped back with forced cheerfulness.

Horace waggled his eyebrows. "Maybe you can model them for me at a more reasonable hour next time? Say…after dark?"

I snorted abruptly. "In your dreams, Horace. Now, if you'll excuse me—"

The sudden groan of a chair leg giving way sent my cup flying from my grasp as if it had grown wings of its own. Hot coffee splattered across the deck like abstract art gone wrong.

"Fiddlesticks!" I yelped, jumping from the broken chair and back from the caffeinated splash zone. Alfie launched from my lap with a yowl.

Horace's laughter boomed from over the fence, his enjoyment clear as day. "Oh, Carrigan! That was gold!"

My face flushed hotter than the spilled brew at my feet. "Yeah? Well, you're about as funny as a fart in an elevator."

With a huff, I grabbed a nearby rag to mop up the mess. My heart pounded in sync with each dab at the liquid—more from irritation than exertion.

"You sure know how to make a gal's morning," I muttered under my breath.

"Oh, sweetheart, you have no idea!" Horace chuckled.

I straightened up and glared over at him with hands on hips. "Be off with you, nosy Sir Horace," I said through gritted teeth.

His laughter subsided into chuckles as he backed away from the fence with an exaggerated bow. "As you wish, Lady Carrigan. Have a delightful day!"

With one last wave and a mischievous grin, he disappeared from view.

I let out a long sigh and sat gingerly on an unbroken chair, trying to regain some semblance of decorum.

"There's never a dull moment," I mumbled to Alfie as he cautiously approached again. He sniffed at the coffee-stained deck before hopping onto my lap with comforting purrs. Alfie settled in, seemingly unfazed by our neighborly interruption or my clumsy antics. I leaned back once more into the chair's precarious embrace. I closed my eyes briefly—noting that maybe today wouldn't be so bad after all—except for losing half a cup of perfectly excellent coffee and exposing my morning disarray to Horace yet again.

Ah well...as long as there were spirits to chat with and mysteries to unravel, life would always be full...even if it meant dealing with nosey neighbors and unexpected showers of java along the way.

———

Thank you for reading!
If you enjoyed this book, please leave a review on your favorite retailer!

The hilarity and hiccups continue with
The Corpse Collector Book 2: Bodies and Bridezilla.

"Ghost Whisperer Carrigan Critt is thrust into a high-stakes mystery when someone turns up dead at the much-anticipated wedding of heiress and Bridezilla, Gabriella St. Claire. As Carrigan navigates the bride's demands and the tangled web of secrets and lies surrounding the wedding party, she relies on her unique ability to communicate with the dead to uncover clues. Balancing humor and suspense, Carrigan's investigation reveals hidden relationships and financial woes, leading her to unmask the cunning murderer before Bridezilla herself becomes a victim."

Other Books in this series: https://payhip.com/tammytyree

Get access to all book bonuses and more in The Vault!

This enchanted corner of Tammy Tyree's magical universe is reserved for our most cherished readers—*newsletter subscribers.*

Inside The Vault, you'll unlock exclusive treasures like free short stories, bonus chapters, and compelling extras from your favorite characters. Subscribe to the newsletter and discover what awaits behind the enchanted door!

https://tammy-tyree.kit.com/2cc3220f59

ACKNOWLEDGMENTS

I want to express my gratitude to my youngest daughter, Carrigan, a real-life 'Corpse Collector' whose candor and appreciation for her work inspired this series.

Also, thank you to my oldest daughter, Chloe, for partnering with me in the book business, and infusing the hilarious moments into this series—several of which are based on her own amusing foibles. Your humor is infectious!

And many thanks to the actress and comedian Miranda Hart, for just being you—my inspiration for 'Carrigan Critt.'

CROCHET TRIXIE'S RAINBOW SKIRT!

This adorable skirt pattern is compliments of www.krazykab-bage.com.

Yarn Bee Sugarwheel Cotton (light weight; 100% cotton) in City Beat. 650 yards.

You will need crochet hook size 7 – 4.5mm and a yarn needle to weave in ends.

Gauge: 12 single crochet x 17 rows = 4".

This pattern uses US terminology.

Stitches and Terms Used: Chain (ch), single crochet (sc), half double crochet (hdc), double crochet (dc), back loop only (blo)

Construction: The skirt is worked sideways in rows as one piece then closed at the seam. This pattern is a 4-row repeat.

This skirt can be made shorter or longer by adding or subtracting a multiple of 12 from the foundation chain.

The waist size can be altered by changing the number of rows.

Start with a slip knot and chain 94. (add multiples of 12 for longer length)

Row 1: Starting in 2nd chain from hook, sc in each of first 10. Hdc in next. 3 dc in next. Dc in each of next 3. *[ch 1, skip 1, dc in next] 3 times. Dc in each of next 6. Repeat from * across until 6 chains remain. [ch 1, skip 1, dc in next] 3 times. At end of row, ch 2 and turn.

Row 2: Working in BLO, Dc in first dc. *[ch 1, skip 1, dc in next] 3 times. Dc in each of next 6. Repeat from * across until 21 stitches remain. [ch 1, skip 1, dc in next] 3 times. Dc in each of next 4. 3 dc in next. Hdc in next. Sc in each of last 10. Ch 1 and turn.

Row 3: BLO. Sc in each of first 10. Hdc in next. 3 dc in next. Dc in each of next 3. *[ch 1, skip 1, dc in next] 3 times. Dc in each of next 6. Repeat from * across until last 10. [ch 1, skip 1, dc in next] 3 times. Dc in each of last 4. Ch 2 and turn.

Row 4: BLO. Dc in each of first 5. *[ch 1, skip 1, dc in next] 3 times. Dc in each of next 6. Repeat from * across until 21 stitches remain. [ch 1, skip 1, dc in next] 3 times. Dc in each of next 4. 3 dc in next. Hdc in next. Sc in each of last 10. Ch 1 and turn.

Row 5: BLO. Sc in each of first 10. Hdc in next. 3 dc in next. Dc in each of next 3. *[ch 1, skip 1, dc in next] 3 times. Dc in each of next 6. Repeat from * across until last 14. [ch 1, skip 1, dc in next] 3 times (leaving 8 open stitches) Ch·2 and turn.

Repeat rows 2-5 until desired waist measurement is reached. On last repeat stop at the end of row 4. Chain 1 and turn.

Fold the skirt over to align the with the foundation chain. Slip stitch through both thicknesses to seam the skirt.

ABOUT THE AUTHOR

Tammy Tyree is a retired Board Certified Clinical Hypnotherapist and award-winning author of paranormal suspense and memoir.

Tammy works with International Bestselling author Carissa Andrews to elevate the lives of aspiring authors and help them achieve millionaire author careers.

When she's not working, Tammy is a devoted mother to four adult children and a doting grandmother to one incredibly perfect granddaughter, whom she loves to spoil.

You can follow Tammy on Facebook and Instagram and visit her website at https://payhip.com/tammytyree

Chloe Hale, a fresh voice in the literary world, brings a delightful sense of humor to her novels. New to writing, she infuses her work with a special charm that captivates readers. When she's not crafting stories, Chloe enjoys crocheting, being outdoors, and spending quality time with her family, especially her lively 5-year-old daughter. An avid reader herself, Chloe draws inspiration from the world around her, making her an exciting new author to watch.

facebook.com / TammyTyreeBooks

instagram.com / tammytyreeauthor

bookbub.com / profile / tammy-tyree

www.ingramcontent.com/pod-product-compliance
Lightning Source LLC
Chambersburg PA
CBHW021219170726
47994CB00013BA/243